Doom and Bloom

A Myrtle Clover Cozy Mystery, Volume 23

Elizabeth Spann Craig

Published by Elizabeth Spann Craig, 2023.

This is a work of fiction. Similarities to real people, places, or events are entirely coincidental.

DOOM AND BLOOM

First edition. November 30, 2023.

Written by Elizabeth Spann Craig.

Chapter One

"It's a travesty," said Myrtle.

Miles gazed down at the rosebush Myrtle was gesturing at. "It does appear to be nibbled on."

"I was quite fond of this rosebush, Miles. I've dead-headed its blooms. I've assiduously shaken Japanese beetles from its branches. I've devotedly watered it. And then this happens on the very day I was going to take pictures and show everyone at the flower show."

Miles decided the best approach was to look on the bright side. "At least you didn't enter it in the juried show."

Myrtle was not prepared to look on the bright side yet. "If I *had* entered it, I would have won. And I'd have taken the blooms and prepared them for an arrangement yesterday. It would have worked out very well."

Miles stared at the nibbled bush. "Deer, I suppose."

"Of course. And what's more, they're Erma's pet deer. The blasted things."

Erma Sherman lived in-between Myrtle and Miles. Myrtle believed her to be one small step above evil incarnate.

Miles blinked at her. "Erma doesn't have pet deer."

"Tell that to Erma. She's the one who feeds the things deer corn. She's also named them ridiculous names that any self-respecting deer would be embarrassed over."

Miles said, "Like Rudolph?"

"Don't be silly, Miles. That's a reindeer name. And she didn't choose Bambi, either. She went in a completely bizarre direction, well-suited to Erma. *Lullaby*, *Jellybean*, and *Snickerdoodle*."

Miles frowned at this. "Those names seem incompatible with wild deer."

"Precisely. Just as Erma is incompatible with polite company. And now her pet deer have ruined my lovely rosebush's photo opportunity. What's worse, I'm going to have to spend part of my day avoiding Erma's company." Myrtle made a face.

"She's going to the garden show?"

"Naturally. Erma does whatever she can to follow me around and make my life miserable."

Miles looked pleased. "I'm even happier that I decided not to attend your garden club's flower show."

"And I'm still peeved you're not coming. But at least Wanda is coming along. You know how Wanda loves these garden club events. I only wish she'd entered something in the show. I believe she could win something," said Myrtle.

Wanda was a friend of both Myrtle and Miles as well as, in a strange twist of fate, Miles's cousin. She lived in a ramshackle house with her brother, Crazy Dan, way off in the country.

"But isn't it judged on the arranging, as well? I'm not sure flower arranging is really in Wanda's wheelhouse."

Myrtle said, "Which is why today will be so helpful for her. One program is on flower arranging. I'm sure Wanda will be avidly listening and scrawling down notes in her very own shorthand."

"How is Wanda getting here, by the way? Do I need to pick her up?"

Myrtle shook her head. "Not today, you don't. Crazy Dan is trying to make amends with Wanda for some sort of wrongdoing. He'll be dropping her off here any minute."

Sure enough, there was a cacophony of backfiring and gears scraping in the street outside. Myrtle smiled. "That must be him now. Let's head back inside."

By the time they walked through the house and reached Myrtle's front door, Wanda was standing on the doorstep, smiling shyly at them. Crazy Dan took his disreputable vehicle off in a cloud of exhaust smoke.

"Mornin'," said Wanda. "Ready for the show?"

"Ready with bells on," said Myrtle. "What's more, I'm feeling very lucky."

"Perhaps you should make a detour to the gas station and purchase lottery tickets," said Miles dryly.

Myrtle gave him a sweet smile. "Perhaps *you* should make a detour, you mean. We'll need a ride to the flower show."

Miles frowned. "Somehow, I didn't get the memo on that. Let me get my car keys."

Wanda turned toward the front door, just as Miles was about to exit. "Watch out."

But Miles must have been too intent on making his way out the door. The streak of black fur that represented Myrtle's feral cat Pasha made him gasp.

"Pasha!" said Myrtle lovingly. "My little darling."

Pasha rubbed up against Myrtle, shooting Miles a reproachful look as he quickly left. Then Pasha padded over to see Wanda. Wanda perched on the edge of the sofa, and Pasha leaped up into her lap, looking up into Wanda's face. Myrtle could swear the cat was smiling.

"Good gurl," murmured Wanda, rubbing the black cat's fur.

"Although the timing could be better," fretted Myrtle. "We're just about to leave the house, and I'm not sure when we'll make it back home."

"Mebbe leave a winda open?"

Myrtle beamed. "Yes. I'll put out a can of tuna, since it's a special day. And I'll keep the kitchen window open so Miss Pasha can jump in and out at will. A brilliant idea, Wanda."

Myrtle had just finished making preparations for Pasha when there was a light toot of the horn outside. "That's our signal," she said.

Myrtle and Wanda clambered into Miles's sedan. He said, "Now, where's the flower show again?"

"In the recreation center," said Myrtle promptly. "The same place you have your chess tournaments." She looked curiously at Miles. "Have you had any chess tournaments lately?"

Miles suddenly looked pleased with himself. "As a matter of fact, I did have one last weekend. I did quite well this time. And I'll be playing again on Tuesday for the chess club, although it's not a tournament."

"Practicing with a computer really makes a difference, does it?" asked Myrtle.

"I suppose so. It's never quite as satisfying when I beat the computer, though. I always have the feeling it's letting me off easy. Letting me win. It makes the whole thing sort of dreary."

"You're the one setting the difficulty level. The *programmer* is the one who's limiting the computer—the computer can't do that on its own," said Myrtle.

Miles glanced over at Myrtle, who was sitting in the passenger seat. "You seem to know an awful lot about computers."

She sniffed. "I know an awful lot about many things. It's just that I may not know about a lot of things in depth."

Miles said, "And you know you feel lucky today."

Wanda made some worried sounds in the backseat, and Miles looked anxiously at her in the rear-view mirror. "Are you all right back there, Wanda? Not feeling carsick, are you?"

Miles, who was already driving rather slowly, slowed his speed even more, apparently concerned about having his seat cushions ruined.

"Not carsick," said Wanda.

Myrtle turned around in her seat to look at Wanda. "Is something going to happen at the flower show?"

"I'm jest getting' some bad vibes, that's all."

Wanda's bad vibes weren't the same as other people's bad vibes. Wanda was a psychic. Her bad vibes could mean anything from a pop-up thunderstorm to a medical emergency in the middle of the venue.

"But you are gonna be lucky," she drawled.

Myrtle puffed up. "That's what I thought."

Miles's voice was uneasy as he said, "Perhaps I shouldn't drop you ladies off. We could have a very nice day at the house watching *Tomorrow's Promise* and playing cards. I did so poorly at hearts the last time we played that I need another opportunity to redeem myself."

"Not today," said Myrtle briskly. "We're going to that flower show. I wanted to attend before, but now I'm positively intrigued by the possibilities of things going haywire. Perhaps Tippy will have a wardrobe malfunction. Or the prize-winning flower arrangement will be unceremoniously dropped by its owner." Her eyes were gleeful at the possibilities.

"Sounds like fun," said Miles dryly. He paused. "What sort of event do you foresee, Wanda?"

"Don't know. Don't look good, though."

Miles said, "I'm not sure how your sense of foreboding and Myrtle's sense of luckiness will intersect. I'm curious to hear about it. What time should I plan on picking you up?"

"Well, the programs and whatnot will go on for a couple of hours. The exhibits are open before and after the programs. Maybe three hours?" Myrtle glanced back at Wanda for approval, and Wanda nodded.

"Got it. I'll do that, then. You can call me if you get tired out before the three hours are up. I have nothing else going on today."

Myrtle was indignant. "For heaven's sake! Wanda and I can handle strolling around a flower show for a few hours. We're both in excellent shape."

Myrtle, certainly, was in good shape. She was built like old farm stock: tall and big-boned. Wanda, however, looked rather like a large gust of wind might blow her to the land of Oz.

Miles knew when to keep quiet. He dutifully drove them to the event and straight up to the drop-off area at the front while Myrtle and Wanda chitchatted about flowers, shrubs, and the upcoming programs.

"Have fun," said Miles as they got out of the car. Myrtle gave him a jaunty wave, and Wanda a gap-toothed smile.

They walked into the event which Myrtle had pre-paid for. "There's Tippy," said Myrtle, looking over at a long table on the way into the exhibit. "Look, she's selling raffle tickets of some sort. Excellent! As lucky as I'm feeling, I'll purchase two of them."

Wanda said, "Jest buy one."

Myrtle raised her eyebrows. "Am I *that* lucky today, then?"

Wanda nodded.

"Perhaps I should have played the lottery after all," mused Myrtle.

Myrtle strode right up to Tippy, nearly plowing over an elderly woman in between them.

Tippy smiled at her. "Want to buy a few raffle tickets, Myrtle?"

Myrtle winked at Wanda. "Actually, I only want to buy a single raffle ticket."

"You'll increase your chances if you buy a few more," said Tippy in her most persuasive voice. "It's for a good cause."

"What's the cause?" asked Myrtle.

"Garden club," said Tippy complacently. "To get more speakers. And perhaps to have a better year-end wrap-up party."

Myrtle wasn't completely sure garden club qualified as a good cause. Besides, she already paid dues to the group and was a widowed retired schoolteacher on an ever-present budget. "Just the same, I'll get the single ticket. But I'll be sure to mention the raffle to everyone I see."

"Perfect," said Tippy, sliding her the ticket after Myrtle paid her. "Be sure to listen to the opening speech. The winner will be announced then."

"Mmm-hmm," said Myrtle, already distracted by the exhibits she could see further in the room. She also knew she'd already won the raffle, so the details didn't bother her much.

"Wouldn't you like to know what the prize is?" asked Tippy.

"I'm sure it will be some sort of gardening tools," said Myrtle. She didn't really care what she won for her dollar. She simply liked the idea of winning something.

Tippy looked slightly deflated. "Yes, they're gardening tools. Excellent gardening tools."

Wanda gave her a sympathetic grin, as if knowing Tippy was a bit disappointed at not getting oohs and ahhs from the description of the prize.

Tippy, accordingly, smiled back. "You don't know how pleased I am to see you here, Wanda. You're always so attentive during the talks. Our speakers have mentioned that to me in past programs. It's so rewarding for them to have an audience member hanging on their every word."

Wanda gave her a shy smile in return. Tippy said, "Have you entered anything in the exhibit?"

Wanda now looked slightly alarmed. "Ain't got money fer garden club."

Tippy now had a determined air about her. "I believe the club can grant a scholarship for your dues."

"Wouldn't wanna cause no trouble," said Wanda, looking down at her scuffed shoes.

"No trouble at all," said Tippy firmly. "Consider it done. Here, take a program with you."

Wanda and Myrtle walked farther into the recreation center. "That were nice of her," said Wanda slowly.

"Oh, you've made Tippy's day. There's nothing she likes better than a project and since the flower show is over today, she needs something new on her agenda. What's more, you've also saved me in the process."

Wanda looked quizzically at Myrtle.

"If you hadn't become Tippy's new project, she'd likely have become ensnared by Red again. Red always wheedles her into volunteering me for various things."

"Thought she'd be busy enough with the town council stuff."

"You'd think," said Myrtle. "But she never seems to feel busy enough. I suspect that Tippy is trying to escape her husband, Benton."

"He's a bad guy?" asked Wanda.

"He's simply unbearably boring. And much worse since he retired from politics himself. Never get the man started on the subject of golf. But we should get on to more pleasant topics. Like flowers. What would you like to see first?" Myrtle looked at her program. "Scented herbs? Potted plants? Arrangements? Horticulture? Bonsai? Orchids?"

Wanda looked at her Timex watch. "Think we should hear the opening speech?"

Myrtle made a face. "You're probably right, although I detest the opening speeches. It's an opportunity for any local blowhard to run their mouth. However, I do want to hear the dulcet tones of my name being voiced by Tippy as the raffle winner. And I suppose they'll be announcing the winners of the various divisions of the exhibit."

They walked into the large center room of the recreation center. There was a lingering scent of popcorn from the movie night a couple of evenings ago. The polished wood floors gleamed. Rows of neatly arranged folding chairs stretched across the open space, facing a modest stage where Tippy stood, looking nervous.

"Gracious, Tippy's not the sort to get stage fright. That's most unlike her. She absolutely adores being up in front of people."

Wanda looked thoughtfully at the anxious Tippy. "Is she the only one talkin'?"

Myrtle peered at her program. "Actually, no. An excellent point, Wanda. She's supposed to be simply introducing the judge. Then the judge, Hortense Winston, is supposed to make a speech."

Wanda looked at her Timex again. "Reckon the judge is runnin' late, then."

"She certainly is. Perhaps she got held up trying to find an acceptable entry for the gardenia category. Those shrubs are very temperamental, you know. If you don't give it exactly what it wants, its leaves will yellow."

"Sounds like trouble," said Wanda.

"Gardenias are trouble, for sure. But they smell glorious. It's unfortunate that they'll fall victim to mildew, stem canker, and root rot at the slightest provocation."

They focused their attention again on the stage. Tippy, always very prompt, now appeared in an agony of indecision about what to do. The judge wasn't available. But everyone was waiting for the program to begin. Finally, she squared her shoulders and walked over to the lectern.

Tippy cleared her throat. "Welcome, everyone, to the tenth annual Bradley Flower Show!"

There was a polite round of applause. Tippy appeared to be looking desperately around her for signs of the absent judge. Seeing none, she cleared her throat once more. "Before we hear from our grand judge today, let's announce the winner of today's raffle prize."

Tippy approached a fishbowl full of tickets, stuck her hand in the bowl, and fished around while looking in the other direction as if there might be a way to cheat.

"Today's winning ticket is 578904," said Tippy, looking expectantly into the audience.

Myrtle coolly stood up. "Bingo," she said.

There was another round of applause, this one perhaps less polite and more envious.

Tippy grinned at her. "Myrtle Clover! Come on up and claim your prize."

Myrtle had the feeling as she thumped her way down the aisle with her cane that Tippy intended to use her to kill time until the judge could be retrieved from the snack bar or the restroom or wherever else she'd gone.

Tippy gave her a perfunctory hug. "Here's your prize, Myrtle. Thanks for supporting garden club."

Myrtle gritted her teeth as she looked into the gift bag. Her prize was a set of ergonomic garden tools for the arthritic. Myrtle was quite proud of her lack of arthritis and her overall health. "Thank you," she growled.

Tippy seemed unaware of any hostility on Myrtle's end. "I know most of us here have known you for a long time, Myrtle. Plenty in the room were actually *taught* by you."

There was a round of applause from the audience. Myrtle acknowledged it with a smile. However, she would not give a monologue about her life in order to use up time before the tardy judge wandered onto the stage. "That's correct."

Tippy, who was possibly not the most creative person in the world, looked desperately at Myrtle. It was completely apparent that she had no idea what to say next.

Myrtle sighed, taking pity on her. She leaned over the microphone. "I believe our audience might want to hear more about the general history of our club, the makeup of its current members, and the kinds of activities we have."

Tippy brightened. Using her unexpected pulpit to expound on and promote the wonders of garden club would be easy for her. Myrtle took this opportunity to escape with her ergonomic garden tools.

When Myrtle reached Wanda, she gestured to the door at the back of the auditorium. Wanda nodded and joined her as Tippy talked about the 1920s and the origins of Bradley's garden club.

"Thank heavens we got out of there," said Myrtle. "Now, what shall we see first? Have you looked at the program?"

Wanda's literacy was tenuous at best, but the program had, obligingly, included pictures of the various exhibits.

"Mebbe the roses?" she asked in a tentative voice.

"An excellent choice. Also, we'll have practically the entire flower show to ourselves since the attendees are trapped in there with Tippy. Let's take advantage of the lack of crowds."

It was indeed uncrowded. In fact, the halls were all but deserted except for a custodian diligently sweeping a stretch of flooring.

"Not feelin' good about this," muttered Wanda.

"What? I thought you wanted to see the roses."

"Not feelin' good about what might happen." She paused, looking toward another corridor in the maze-like recreation center.

"Something's wrong down there? Is this related to that uneasy feeling you had in the car? The one that Miles was so quick to write off as motion sickness?"

Wanda nodded.

"Well then, I think I should take a look. We do, after all, have an AWOL judge. I'm wondering if there might be a good reason for that." She looked at her program. "This hallway is the horticulture division. With 'a dazzling variety of genus, species, and cultivars.'"

Wanda stared down the hallway as if the horticulture division encompassed unseen horrors.

"I'll just nip down and see what I can see. You stay put, and I'll be right back in a jiffy."

But Wanda, despite her foreboding, wasn't going to allow Myrtle to venture toward the horticulture division by herself. She loped next to her, eyes alert.

Myrtle walked into the exhibit and stopped. She turned to Wanda. "You were right."

The flower show judge lay sprawled on the floor, mouth agape as if in surprise. A broken clay flowerpot lay next to her.

Chapter Two

"Do you know her?" breathed Wanda.

Myrtle nodded, looking down at the reedy figure on the floor. "She's Dr. Hortense Winston. The missing judge for the event." She carefully put a finger on where Hortense's pulse should be and shook her head. The florescent lights from above lent an almost clinical feel to the scene.

"Wuz she a nice person?"

Myrtle pursed her lips. "I wouldn't say she was the nicest person, no. She was quite passionate about gardening, though. I'm not sure she cared much for people, however. I suppose I should call Red and alert him."

"He's not here at the show?"

Myrtle said, "It's not Red's scene at all. He might have helped with traffic control if there was a need, but this is Bradley. Fifty cars in a vast parking lot were completely manageable." She glanced around her. "Unfortunately, I don't immediately see any clues to identify the perpetrator, do you, Wanda?"

Wanda peered around the room. "Jest that the flowerpot wuz the weapon."

"Right. Someone slammed it into her head. I find it difficult to believe that it would be because Hortense gave the killer's horticulture exhibit a low score." She sighed, taking her cell phone out of her large pocketbook.

Red, her son and the town's police chief, answered immediately. "What's going on, Mama? Everything okay?"

"Sadly, everything is not okay. I'm over at the flower show."

Red growled, "Are you still upset that your rosebush was eaten up by Erma's deer? I told you there's nothing I can do about that. It's hardly grounds for an arrest. Now listen, I have some paperwork I've gotta take care of."

"You're about to have a lot more paperwork. There's a body here."

There was silence on the other end. "Are you talking about a human body?"

"Of course I'm talking about a human body. It's in the horticulture division. I'm assuming you'll want to shut down the event and secure the venue. Considering there are quite a few people here and that Tippy is likely running out of ways to stall them from running rampant around the rec center, I figured you'd want to head over here right away."

"Coming right over," said Red grimly. "Mama? Be safe. Get away from the body and the area."

"Oh, I have Wanda with me for protection."

The sigh that Red gave before hanging up the phone indicated he didn't think much about Wanda's capacity as a bodyguard.

Just then, there was a buzz of voices coming down the hallway. "Tippy must have finally run out of things to say," said Myrtle. "We have to protect the crime scene, Wanda."

Myrtle bustled out of the horticulture exhibit and toward the general noise coming toward them. In her most effective teacher's voice, she bellowed, "STOP."

Most people did stop, perhaps to stare and wonder why the elderly woman seemed to be so agitated. Some people, perhaps determined to find out if their Mr. Lincoln red rose had won its category, pressed on.

Myrtle did not take kindly to being thwarted. She reached out for the light switch and clicked it off, sending the entire enclosed hallway into darkness.

Now the general noise sounded more alarmed. Myrtle's voice rose above the din. "Attention! Everyone must turn around and exit the building. There has been an incident and the police are on the way."

There was a bit of hesitation with some people lingering and some, perhaps eager to be back in some form of light again, turned and started moving toward the exit.

"Now!" encouraged Myrtle.

"We gonna join 'em?" asked Wanda.

"Absolutely not. We're going to guard the crime scene until Red strings up his yellow crime scene tape. We must find out who killed poor Hortense, even if no one seemed very fond of her." Myrtle's eyes narrowed. "The very idea of anyone sullying my garden club's event with murder! It's outrageous."

Wanda nodded sadly. "I were lookin' forward to the programs."

"With any luck, Tippy will have enough funds in the budget to rent the rec center again and reschedule," said Myrtle. "Otherwise, perhaps the speakers will be kind enough to attend a series of regular club meetings. Even remotely."

The sound of a siren broke into her musings. "Finally," said Myrtle rather waspishly. "That took forever."

Wanda looked at her Timex, noting it had been a matter of five minutes, but wisely kept that knowledge to herself.

There was a bit of shouting outside. "That will be Red, repeating my instructions to stay clear of the building," said Myrtle.

"Reckon it's time fer us to leave, too. Crime scene protector's on his way."

"Let's just stay until he comes down the hall."

Which was momentarily. Red's face was just as red as his hair as he stomped toward them. "I didn't want you anywhere near this crime scene," he huffed at Myrtle.

Myrtle said coldly, "I was sure you didn't want anyone *else* near this crime scene. And there was a veritable horde descending on it until I turned them away."

Red muttered. "Hordes. In Bradley."

"Precisely," said Myrtle with a sniff.

"Okay. Well, now you can head out the door. Thank you, Mama."

Myrtle, pleased at being asked nicely for once, sailed toward the closest exit, with Wanda in tow.

As soon as they got outside the recreation center, everyone was looking their way. Clearly, they were the ones who knew what was going on and why the police had turned up at a flower show.

Tippy was the first to reach them. She was pale and there was a tightness around her lips. "Myrtle? Did something happen?" She paused and asked in a quieter voice. "Does it have something to do with Hortense?"

Myrtle gave a bob of her head. "I'm afraid so, Tippy. But I suppose we should have guessed that Hortense had met some sort of horrid fate. She wasn't the type of person to shy away from a lectern, was she?"

Tippy looked deflated. "No, she wasn't." She glanced around them at the interested faces that were hoping to glean information. She lowered her voice once again, and Myrtle reflected it was good she had such excellent hearing for her age. "Did she have a medical emergency? A heart attack? A terrible stroke?"

Tippy wasn't one to be ghoulish over death, and Myrtle knew she simply hoped that an act of violence hadn't desecrated the garden club's flower show. But Myrtle had to shake her head. "I'm afraid not. It was definitely foul play. But Wanda and I can't disclose more information than that, of course."

Tippy gave a long sigh. "Oh no. So the event will need to be closed down for the day."

"I'm sure. It's quite a large crime scene, isn't it? A whole recreation center."

Tippy quietly said, "I heard from the attendees that it was near the horticulture division."

Since there were going to be many people who'd attest to that fact, Myrtle nodded.

Tippy gave another long sigh, as if the horticulture division was positively the worst location for a homicide. But she'd likely have had the same reaction if it had been in the roses or any of the other exhibits. She turned to Wanda. "Wanda, what happened?"

Wanda looked a bit startled. "Ain't did nothin'," she said. Her pale face was even paler than usual.

"Of course you didn't! The very idea, Tippy," said Myrtle with great hostility.

Tippy reflexively put her hands up in protection from Myrtle's wrath. "Sorry, that was poorly worded, Wanda. I only meant, with your amazing abilities, do you have any insight into this awful event?"

Wanda looked sadly at Tippy, then turned to Myrtle to give her a beseeching look.

"The Sight doesn't work that way," said Myrtle briskly.

Wanda nodded in agreement.

"I see," said Tippy slowly. "Thanks, Wanda. And I'm very sorry we're having to cancel today's event. I know you were probably looking forward to it."

Myrtle said, "I was wondering if the speakers could either come to our regular meetings, or if they could do a zoom presentation instead. It was an excellent lineup that you'd planned. It seems a pity for the speakers not to give their talks."

"Good idea, Myrtle. I'll contact the presenters and see if that might work for them. I'm sure they've all gotten lost in the chaos, so I'll have to email them later. Although I will certainly look at our budget and see if we might simply reschedule the flower show for a later date." Someone called Tippy's name, and she quickly said, "I'd best go. See you ladies later."

Wanda shivered, despite the warmth of the day. "Wanda, we should get you out of here before you get swamped by middle-aged women wanting fortunes. I'll give Miles a call."

"Won't Red wanna talk to me?"

Myrtle frowned. "Hm. Yes, I suppose he will. But he can find you at my house if I tell him that's where you'll be. Here's a key." She dropped her house key into Wanda's bony hand and then fished out her cell phone. "Miles? Yes, it's early. No, things have gone haywire, much as Wanda predicted. Could you run by and pick her up? I think this has all been a bit much for her."

Myrtle listened and then said, "Got it. Thanks." She turned to Wanda. "Miles will pick you up at the front, where he dropped us off. He'll be here in 10 minutes."

Wanda nodded, looking exhausted. Myrtle said, "Why don't you head that way now? There are benches you can sit on there, and it's shady. We're right in the sun here, and there's no point in standing when you can sit."

"What about you?"

Myrtle said stoutly, "I'm just fine. Besides, I want to poke around here a little and see if I can find something out."

"Be careful."

Myrtle smiled at her. "Yes, I know. I'm in danger."

"Yep. From Erma."

Myrtle looked a lot more alarmed by the possibility of her vexatious neighbor than the prospect of a murderer. "Oh heavens. Is she on the prowl? Okay, I'll watch out for her."

Wanda slipped away to meet up with Miles just as Red came out of the building, speaking in a clipped voice to someone on his phone. His eyes locked on Myrtle's as he hung up his phone.

He gestured her to come up to the doorway, where they could chat in a bit of privacy.

"Where's Wanda?" he asked, glancing around the crowd of flower show attendees.

Myrtle waved her hand in the air to indicate Wanda had evaporated.

"Gone?" Red frowned. "In a poof, like Glinda, the good fairy?"

"Not in a poof, in a car. Or she soon will be, at any rate. I sent her back to my house. Finding bodies is most distressing for her."

"But not for you," said Red heavily. "Because you're so very adept at it."

"Now, Red. You make it sound as if I do nothing but stumble over bodies. Or that I'm somehow complicit in arranging them to be stumbled over in the first place. All I was doing was escaping the painful process of hearing Tippy at the microphone, trying desperately to fill dead time."

Red cocked his head to one side. "I'm not following you."

"It's very simple. The woman back in the horticulture division is Hortense Winston. She's the judge for the flower show—or was. She was scheduled to give a talk after Tippy introduced her this morning. However, Hortense didn't show."

"And I'm guessing you decided to investigate," said Red, rolling his eyes.

"Not at all. I figured Hortense had lost track of time or was visiting the ladies' room or something. After winning my raffle prize, I simply wanted to spare Wanda and myself from the onslaught of Tippy making up a speech as she went along. Tippy is very impressive at extraneous speaking, but even she has her limits. Wanda and I were heading off to see the rose exhibit while everyone else was listening to Tippy."

Red asked, "At what point did you realize something was wrong?"

"When Wanda started getting a terrible feeling."

"Wanda was sick?" asked Red.

"Wanda knew that a dreadful tragedy had occurred. It was easy enough to intuit what the tragedy was, considering the AWOL judge. And just as easy to locate the location."

Red was about to delve further into Hortense's discovery when they were suddenly interrupted by Martha Green, one of the former garden club presidents. She and Tippy tended to trade the presidential office back and forth between themselves. Martha, like Tippy, cut a very elegant appearance. But unlike Tippy, Myrtle could always picture Martha pulling weeds and digging in the dirt. In honor of the flower show, Martha was wearing a floral dress, accessorized with a vintage brooch of a rose.

Red raised an eyebrow at the interruption. "Martha? The state police and I will come around to speak with everyone in due time."

Martha was a few years older than Red and not at all cowed by being told by the police chief to go away. "Hi there, Red. I need to update our guests at the flower show. Everyone is getting quite restless. And I fear water might be required for some of them."

"It's only been a few minutes," said Red. "I'm sure they can wait. The state police are on the way. But while you're here, I'll have a word with you now."

Myrtle was delighted that Red seemed to forget she was there for the moment. Perhaps it was because she'd taken a couple of steps back and was pretending to be very interested in a loud conversation behind her. Red always underestimated her hearing. Myrtle's hearing was excellent.

"So you're the current garden club president, is that right?" asked Red.

"Not currently, no. Tippy and I swap the position between ourselves, and Tippy is up right now. However, Tippy had to deliver a monologue for thirty minutes when Hortense didn't show, and she's rather tapped out right now. I'm stepping in for the time being."

Red took out a small notebook and a stub of a pencil from his front pocket of his uniform. "All right," he said. "If you could, please tell me the last time you saw Hortense."

"I suppose it was when I opened the door for her to come into the rec center this morning. It was before the event opened to the public. We needed to give Hortense the chance to come in, see the exhibits, and judge them."

Red said, "Right. Makes sense. How did Hortense seem when you saw her?"

"Well, just the same as always. Sort of curt and rude, honestly. But since she's always that way, it's not the sort of thing you find off-putting. She was also in a hurry to get going with the judging."

"Was she the only judge? It seems like there were quite a few categories to judge," said Red.

"There were two other judges. Hortense was the head judge. She was also there to tally up the votes and be the tie-breaker if needed."

Red nodded, making notes in his notebook. "Okay. So are the other judges around, then?"

"No, they judged yesterday. Tippy let them in, they walked around, and they made their choices."

"Got it." Red paused. "And where were you this morning when Hortense went missing?"

Myrtle gave a half-smile. Red had done an excellent job of asking rather mundane questions before inquiring after the alibi.

Martha sounded startled. "Me? I don't know exactly when Hortense went missing. Like I said, the last time I saw her was when she came into the building, long before the public was allowed in." Her peaches and cream complexion was now flushed.

Red patiently asked, "Where were you this morning, then? Up until the point where Hortense didn't show up for speaking?"

"I could have been doing any number of things, Red. I checked on the fundraising booth where the club was selling seed packets, gardening tools, and flower show tee shirts. I also checked on our refreshments booth where our volunteers were selling drinks and snacks. I was flitting around from one thing to the other."

Red nodded, making a note in his notebook. Myrtle knew the note would have made the point that Martha didn't have much of an alibi at all. Instead, she'd been all over the venue. Seen by other people, yes, but it would certainly have been easy for her to murder Hortense and slip back into her role of checking up on things.

"And what did you think of Hortense?" asked Red genially. "I didn't really know her."

Martha gave a sweet smile that seemed fake to Myrtle. "Well, I had a good deal of respect for Hortense."

Red gave her a sweet smile back. "Although you mentioned her being rude and curt."

Martha's pale skin flushed even more. "I was being honest. She *was* rude and curt. But I could see through all that and see her gentle side. Her love of gardening, mainly. Where she might not have had much patience with people, she had tons of patience for plants."

Red frowned. "Do plants need patience?"

"They certainly do. Sometimes people will own plants that give out signs of distress. Maybe their leaves are dropping or turning color. Impatient people won't nurse the poor plants back to life again. They just chuck them in the trash." Martha sounded very indignant about this.

A look of irritation crossed Red's features, and Myrtle suppressed a smile. Red was definitely not interested in hearing a lecture about plants at this moment. He said, "I suppose you must have a deep love of gardening, too? Did you have something on exhibit today?"

Martha nodded eagerly. She fished her phone out of her purse and scrolled until she came to the photo she was looking for. "It's in the arrangements category. It's called 'Enchanted Dreams.'"

Red glanced at the picture and did not give it the attention that Martha clearly wanted him to. Myrtle stepped in. "May I see that photo, dear?"

Martha happily surrendered her phone to Myrtle. Myrtle saw a tall crystal vase filled with delicate strands of what appeared to be LED lights intertwined with transparent water beads. The flowers were sprays of vibrant orchids in hues of white, purple, and fuchsia. Jasmine tendrils, purple heather, and fern fronds intertwined with the orchids.

Martha was looking carefully at Myrtle. Her expression was anxious, as if she was waiting with bated breath to learn what Myrtle thought of the arrangement. Myrtle thought it certainly wasn't Red's cup of tea, as evidenced by his reaction. Nor was it Myrtle's, actually. She was much more of a fan of old-fashioned flower arrangements involving vintage vases, roses, lilies, and baby's breath. But Myrtle smiled and said, "Simply lovely, Martha."

Martha glowed at the compliment.

Myrtle decided it was time to try to draw Martha out. Martha was the sort of woman who knew things. She decided if she spoke of Hortense in a somewhat derogatory way, she might get more of an honest opinion.

"Hortense was rather an odd choice for judge, don't you think? I believe you did a much better job when you judged last year."

Red gave his mother an annoyed look at the interjection. But Martha glowed at the compliment. Myrtle added, "Hortense could be so very critical, couldn't she? I've heard her absolutely eviscerate people before, simply because she had a completely different taste in flowers or arrangements."

Martha nodded eagerly, glad someone apparently shared her views. "That's exactly the way Hortense was. She had a very specific criteria for every arrangement, and it was totally based on her personal preferences."

Myrtle quickly added before Red could hop back in again, "Don't I remember a bit of a contretemps between you and Hortense? Over something Hortense said, of course. She could be so very thoughtless. But I don't think I remember the details."

Martha, however, didn't take the bait this time. In fact, she looked alarmed, most likely because of the presence of the police chief and the fact they were at a murder scene. She simply shook her head and looked away. Red shot his mother an annoyed look.

Red said, "Maybe, Martha, since Hortense was so difficult, you can remember if someone else might be upset with her. It sounds like much of the town could be at odds with her from what I've gathered."

Martha nodded, happily latching onto the theory of suspects other than herself. "Yes. Although I spent little time with Hortense, I remember her saying that she'd recently fired Earl Jenkins."

Red jotted this bit of information down. "Got it. Earl was her landscaper, I'm guessing?"

"That's right. He accidentally killed her prize rose garden," said Martha.

Myrtle said, "What? How does someone kill a rose garden by accident?"

Red shot her yet another annoyed look.

Martha said, "He thought his sprayer had fertilizer in it, but it was full of weedkiller. It was a totally honest mistake. He was devastated when he found out what he'd done. You know what a plant-lover Earl is."

Myrtle did indeed. She would love to be able to afford Earl as a landscaper instead of the lackadaisical Dusty.

Red's gaze latched onto something behind Myrtle. "I'd better speak with my deputy. Martha, thanks for the information. Mama, please head back home and put your feet up."

Martha quickly dissolved into the crowd, and Red suddenly disappeared, as well. Myrtle was trying to decide if she should call Miles or try to glean more information about Hortense from various people at the event when she heard an unwelcome voice behind her.

Chapter Three

"**M**yrtle!"

Myrtle gave a visceral shiver. It was Erma, her much-loathed next-door neighbor. She cursed under her breath. Red had clearly seen Erma coming and deserted her in her hour of need. She was also irritated with herself. Wanda had warned her, after all, and Myrtle hadn't been as vigilant as she'd needed to be to avoid an Erma encounter.

Erma gave Myrtle a leering grin. "I should have known you'd be here. Of course, if there's a body around, Myrtle Clover is right on site." She tilted her head, turning her rat-like features around. "Where's your boyfriend?"

Myrtle gave her a disdainful look. "If you're referring to Miles, he's not here. Nor is he my boyfriend."

Erma brayed in laughter. "I know that. Anyway, what's the scoop on the murder? Who was it? Somebody said Hortense didn't show up to give her speech at the beginning of the show. Is Hortense dead?"

Myrtle pulled herself to her full height of nearly six feet tall. "As you mentioned, it is indeed a scoop. You'll have to wait and read the details in my article tomorrow for the *Bradley Bugle*."

Erma slumped in disappointment. "Really? Because, if it *had* been Hortense, I was going to give you some useful information. Call me Watson to your Sherlock."

Myrtle had no intention of calling Erma any such thing. "What was the useful information? Perhaps it can serve as background info. *If* it's actually useful." Which Myrtle seriously doubted.

Erma grinned at her. "Okay. Well, I heard that Emily White was stealing flowers from Hortense's garden. *Stealing* them." Erma tried her best to look aghast, but only succeeded in looking delighted, instead.

"Emily?" Myrtle frowned. "That charming young woman who works at the diner?" Because she was decidedly charming. But quite the worst server she'd ever experienced. Emily consistently got orders wrong, neglected to refill coffee cups and waters, and never failed to drop things.

"That's right," said Erma, pleased to be the one to tell Myrtle something she didn't know.

"Are we talking about Emily *picking* flowers? Like to create an arrangement of some kind? Because that doesn't really seem like such a terrible crime to me."

Erma's face dropped. "But it is a terrible crime. Hortense was infuriated. And Emily didn't just pick the flowers. She divided them to plant them in her own yard. That's definitely theft."

Myrtle said, "Did Red know about it? Did Hortense report the fact that Emily was trespassing?"

"It wasn't *just* trespassing. It was stealing. And she was going to, for sure. I don't know if she got around to it." Erma gave a dramatic gasp. "What if Emily killed Hortense before she could report her to the police?"

"I wouldn't let my imagination go wild," said Myrtle, irked that perhaps Erma had somehow solved the case before Myrtle had even had a chance to investigate. "Now, I really must go, Erma."

"I need to leave, too. I'll give you a ride."

This displeased Myrtle tremendously. "I'm sure I can get Elaine to pick me up." She was actually going to call Miles once more, but wasn't about to tell Erma that and get Erma leering at her again.

"That's silly. I live right next door to you, and I'm leaving now." Erma herded Myrtle toward the parking lot and then flung open the passenger door, gesturing inside.

Myrtle looked glumly out the window during the short ride home. It had been a very unusual day so far. She'd won an ergonomic garden set when she'd hoped for a more glamorous outcome from her lucky streak. She'd stumbled across a body, which should have introduced an interesting element to her day, but resulted somehow in Erma giving her a ride home.

Erma was chatting blithely away about, from what Myrtle could tell, complete and utter nonsense. "When I saw Tippy before the flower show kicked off, she complimented my outfit. Can you believe it?"

Myrtle could believe that Tippy was being exceedingly kind over the obnoxiously bright floral ensemble Erma was wearing.

"Now I feel like a fashionista! Maybe I can even start being like one of those influencers on social media. Then retailers will send me clothes for *free* just to share them with my audience."

"I wouldn't get too far ahead of myself," muttered Myrtle.

Erma looked pointedly over at Myrtle's own ensemble: sturdy shoes, slacks, and a button-down blouse. "Maybe I can go shopping with you at some point and update *your* wardrobe."

Myrtle shuddered at the idea.

Erma's eyes narrowed when she saw the jaunty gift bag next to Myrtle's leg. "Say! Is it your birthday or something?"

"What? No. Oh, you mean the bag. I won the raffle," said Myrtle. She still felt a lift when she thought about beating everyone else in the recreation center. Although the prize itself was a bit wanting.

"Did you? What did you win? A gift card to the nursery?"

A gift card to the nursery would have been highly preferable. "Some garden tools," said Myrtle carefully.

"Wow, that's really cool." Erma lurched to a stop at the stop sign in downtown Bradley, reached over, and availed herself of the bag.

Myrtle was furious but hadn't been able to tell Erma's intentions before she snagged the gift bag.

Erma brayed with laughter. "Ergonomic tools. Haha! They must have had an inkling you were going to win, Myrtle. Maybe they rigged the whole thing so you *would* win. Haha!"

Myrtle gritted her teeth, against dentist orders.

Finally, the tortuous car ride was over. Myrtle eagerly reached for the passenger door and got herself out. "Thanks, Erma," she said hurriedly.

"My pleasure!" said Erma, saluting her as she rushed to her front door.

Wanda opened the door before she could knock. She gave Myrtle a sympathetic look. "Sorry about Erma."

"You were absolutely right, Wanda. I should never have let my guard down. If I hadn't been so focused on getting clues to Hortense's murder, I'd have seen Erma coming a mile away. Especially considering her horrendously bright outfit."

"Reckon it's over now, anyway," said Wanda, always one to look on the bright side.

"True. And I suppose Erma gave me some helpful information regarding Emily White. She apparently divided some of Hortense's prize plants without permission, and Hortense threatened to call the police on her."

Wanda said, "Sounds like a reason to be killin' somebody."

"Exactly. I just hate it that Erma was helpful. It's most annoying."

Wanda said, "Mebbe if you talk to Emily, you'll git info Erma didn't have."

"An excellent idea, Wanda! And I know just how we'll speak with her. She works at Bo's Diner. She's actually a completely inept waitress, but she seems like a nice girl. We'll invite Miles to go with us. I'm sure you filled him in on the unexpected events of the day?"

Wanda nodded. "He said he figured that's why he didn't wanna go. Said all kinds of shenanigans happen at flower shows."

Myrtle pulled out her phone and rang Miles. He answered, sounding wary. "Myrtle? We're not investigating, are we?"

"For heaven's sake, Miles. Of *course* we are. You're my loyal sidekick. You know how this works. Besides, it will be an easy assignment. We'll eat at the diner. I'll pay for everyone."

Wanda tilted her head to one side. She gave Myrtle a doubtful look.

Miles, on the other end of the phone, also sounded doubtful. "It's nearing the end of the month, Myrtle. Are you sure you want to pay for everyone?"

"Let me consult my checkbook," said Myrtle. She kept a very tidy ledger in there. Now, opening it, she found her funds were quite a bit lower than she'd imagined them to be. She sighed. "Well, I suppose I won't pay for everyone. I had a dental cleaning and the state of my exchequer right now is horrifyingly low."

Miles quickly said, "I'll pay. I do want to hear what happened. Wanda was too tapped out to fill me in very much. I'll be there in three minutes."

On the way to the diner, Myrtle told Miles what happened at the flower show.

"I knew there was a reason I didn't want to attend," muttered Miles.

Myrtle continued on as if there hadn't been an interruption. "So, we'll speak with Emily at the diner."

"Emily, that hapless server?" asked Miles in horror. "She spilled coffee on my favorite pair of khaki pants last time."

"Yes, that Emily. I'm sure she's had more practice since then."

"But that was day-before-yesterday," said Miles.

"Maybe she practices waitressing at home, after hours. At any rate, we do need to speak with her. I want to hear more about this incident that happened at Hortense's house."

Miles was fortunate enough to find parking right in front of the diner. He courteously held the door open as Wanda and Myrtle entered. Even on the most unsettling days, Myrtle felt a sense of continuity as she walked through the door of the diner. The place had been there since Myrtle was little, handed down from one member of the family to the next generation. It sported vinyl booths, laminated menus, and a comforting home-cooked smell. A sign on the wall stated, "the language you use in church is good enough to use in here."

"Seat yourselves!" said Emily cheerfully as she strode by with a couple of plates of food balanced precariously on her arm.

Myrtle chose a booth fairly far away from the door. If they were going to talk about murder, it should be private. Her gaze followed Emily as she bounced around the diner. Emily must have been in her mid-twenties. Her blonde curls cascaded down her shoulders, freckles dotted her cheeks, and her emerald eyes sparkled as she interacted with a group of old men who seemed positively enchanted.

"She's a cute girl," said Myrtle. "However, I don't believe she has much of a future as a server."

As if to prove Myrtle's point, Emily knocked over one of the old men's water glasses. She apologized profusely, sopping up the water with another man's napkin.

Miles grimaced. "I don't really fancy paying for food and having Emily destroy it."

"You know the kitchen will replace the food for free. I think Bo is being very generous to continue employing Emily. But, on to more important matters. What are you both getting to eat?"

Wanda had carefully studied the laminated menu, which accommodated limited literacy by including pictures of the various dishes. She hesitated, clearly not wanting to order too much since she wasn't going to be paying for it. "Mebbe a side order of toast."

Miles glanced over at her. "You've had quite a morning, Wanda. Get something hearty and filling."

She smiled her gap-toothed smile at him. "Whatcha gonna get, Miles?"

"Oatmeal."

Myrtle rolled her eyes. "Not this again. It's not even breakfast time. It's *definitely* lunch time."

"I remember they've been good at serving me oatmeal whenever I ask for it. Besides, *I* didn't have an eventful morning. Plus, I ate a Greek yogurt recently. The diner has been putting brown sugar and cinnamon on it for me, which is a nice touch."

Myrtle made a face. "Well, I'm going to get the pimento cheese and chili dogs with a side of fries."

Now it was Miles's turn to make a face. "I don't know how you end up with such excellent labs at your physicals. Your arteries must be extraordinary."

Myrtle said, "It's because I eat a well-balanced diet. Plus, I make a point to consume a good breakfast every day. With protein!"

Miles sighed. He seemed to know Myrtle was going to pick on his beloved oatmeal again.

Sure enough, Myrtle continued, "You've been on a real oatmeal kick lately, haven't you? Oatmeal certainly has its *place*, but just remember that breakfast is the cornerstone for the day."

Emily sailed over to their table. "Hi guys! Have you decided? Lots of good stuff on the menu, don't you think?"

Miles looked over at Wanda. "Do you know what you want?"

She nodded shyly. "Could I git the meatloaf and gravy with th' mashed potatoes?"

"Excellent choice!" said Emily cheerfully, jotting it down on her order pad. "You get another side with that."

Wanda squinted at her menu again, and Myrtle unobtrusively tapped the correct spot for her.

"Mebbe the buttered carrots."

Emily smiled at her. "Got it. And you folks?"

Myrtle and Miles gave her their orders. Myrtle wanted to speak with Emily, but she also wanted to eat. She decided the best way to get both things to occur was to let Emily place the orders with the kitchen staff before returning to the table.

As Emily scampered off, Miles raised his eyebrows. "You didn't waylay her, Myrtle. I'm surprised."

"I wanted her to get our order in. I've worked up a terrific appetite. Don't worry, I'll flag her down as soon as she returns from the kitchen."

Sure enough, Myrtle waved at Emily shortly after. Emily grinned at her and headed back. "What can I get for y'all?"

Considering the fact they didn't have silverware, waters, or any other beverage, Myrtle would have thought it would be self-evident. But she was nice. "Could we get coffee, waters, and silverware, dear?"

Emily flushed in embarrassment. "Of course you can. I'm sorry. I don't know where my brain is today." She hurried off and came back, a trail of water and coffee in her wake. "Here we are!"

"Thank you," said Myrtle. "And now I have something to tell you. I don't *believe* the news has made the rounds yet, considering how quiet the diner is right now. Hortense Winston is dead."

Fortunately, Emily had put everything that was on her tray on their table, because she dropped the plastic tray with a resounding crash on the floor.

Chapter Four

"You're kidding," she said in a shaky voice.

"I'm afraid not. Wanda and I found her."

Emily's eyes grew enormous. "But today was the flower show. You found her at the flower show?"

Myrtle and Wanda somberly nodded.

"How awful," murmured Emily.

"You knew her, dear, didn't you?" asked Myrtle. "It's just that I've heard a particular rumor. I thought you might be interested in hearing the news."

Now Emily flushed even more. "I knew her, but not in a good way. Oh, I can't believe she's dead."

Absently, Emily lowered herself into the vinyl booth, right next to Miles. This startled Miles, and he blinked a few times before carefully sliding over to provide Emily with a bit more room. The manager, seeing what happened, shook his head and looked annoyed. It was fortunate that the diner was as quiet as it was.

Emily opened her mouth, and the entire story started spilling out. "I know the rumor you're talking about. But you have to believe me; Hortense needed to thin those plants out, anyway. She'd gotten pretty lax on yard maintenance lately, probably because she let her yard guy go. But also because she seemed like she had something on her mind. Anyway, those plants were getting totally choked out. I was doing her a favor by dividing them up and taking a few." Emily was flushed with indignation, not at Myrtle, but at the neglected plants.

"Did Hortense believe you were doing her a favor?" asked Myrtle.

Emily shook her head miserably. Then she started to cry, which made everyone at the table most uncomfortable. Emily reached over, grabbed Miles's napkin, and blew her nose emphatically with it.

"Hortense was *so* angry. I've never seen anyone that mad." She lowered her voice, looking nervously toward the door. "Do you think the police are going to talk to me, Miss Myrtle? Didn't you tell me Red was your son?"

Myrtle nodded. "But I'm afraid I'm quite inept at reading Red's mind. I will say that people in this town seem to trust my son, and they often confide in him. I'd imagine that if he hasn't heard the story about your falling-out with Hortense, he likely will soon."

Emily slumped in the booth. Her manager watched with cold eyes from across the diner. "That's what I was worried about. In a town like Bradley, there aren't any secrets."

Miles cleared his throat. "It sounds to me like a lot of problems would be solved with an effective alibi. Were you working here all morning?"

Emily's eyes filled with tears again. "No, I wasn't. I just came in about thirty minutes ago. I would have loved to have gone to the flower show, but I couldn't afford to buy a ticket. Plus, it kind of annoyed me that Hortense was going to be the grand judge."

Miles said slowly, "Excuse me for prying, but I don't completely understand the issue with Hortense's plants."

Emily said, "Well, I'm a gardening nut. I've always loved being out in the yard with dirt under my nails, pulling weeds and planting things. But now that I'm out in the world and making my own living, I just don't have the money for gardening like I did when I was living with my folks."

"So you . . . resorted to removing plants from Hortense's yard?" he asked a bit awkwardly.

Emily gave him an impish grin through her tears. "I like the way you put that. *Removing.* I might go a step further and say that I was *rescuing* them. I'd been on the garden club tour of homes a couple of years ago, and I saw how gorgeous Hortense's yard was. It was almost like it was a sanctuary for her. I could tell how proud she was of it. When she was touring us around, she was almost glowing with pride."

"I didn't go on that tour," said Myrtle. "But I've heard she has a lovely yard."

"It was amazing. Carolina Jasmine and wisteria vines were climbing on the gate around the yard. She had Pink Lady's Slipper orchids in the shade, and they were in great shape."

Wanda was looking sadly envious. Myrtle made a mental note to include her on the next tour of homes.

Emily continued, "Her Azalea bushes were beautiful. They made it look like her yard was just blazing with color. Then, I was walking by her house the other day and peeked through the fence. It wasn't nearly as well-kept and lovely as it had been. She has these walkways that wind through her garden, and they used to be totally immaculate. But there were some really stubborn-looking weeds taking them over. Just little signs of neglect. The problem was, that she'd fired Earl, of course. Anyway, while I was looking through the fence, I saw a couple of plants that I coveted like crazy. A prize Hosta and a giant fern."

"And you availed yourself of the plants," said Myrtle.

"No, this is where everyone who's spreading the rumor is wrong. I *asked* Hortense, fair and square, if I could divide the plants up. I told her I'd do it myself and would be very careful."

"And she told you yes?" asked Miles.

Wanda shook her head, looking troubled.

"She told me to go ahead. But I should have known I'd run into issues because she was so totally distracted when I talked to her. It was like my words were going in one ear and out through the other."

Myrtle said, "Hortense forgot she'd given you the okay to get the plants?"

"It was like our conversation never even happened. She was *livid* when she saw me digging in her yard." Emily twisted Miles's napkin in her hands. "Oh, my gosh. The cops are going to hear about this and think I killed Hortense."

"What *were* you doing this morning, since you weren't working or at the flower show?" asked Myrtle. "Did you just sleep in?"

"I went to the pollinator garden over at the park. If I can't have a huge garden at home, at least I can see a beautiful one for free at the park. Are you familiar with it?"

Myrtle nodded. "My garden club helps maintain it as one of our volunteer projects."

Emily said, "There's a bench there in front of the garden where I like to sit. Right in front of some milkweed that attracts the monarch butterflies. I guess the stress just got to me because I started boo-hooing right there at the park. A young guy sat next to me and asked if I was okay. I told him the whole story about Hortense and how she got so mad at me for taking the plants." She smiled. "He told me he believed me. But I don't know his name or anything about him. He could be an alibi if I did."

Miles cleared his throat. "If you see him again, ask him for his contact information."

Emily snorted. "He'd probably think I was going to ask him out on a date or something."

Miles flushed a little, clearly not having thought of this possibility.

Myrtle said briskly, "Well, if it keeps you out of jail, it's worth a bit of misunderstanding. Besides, you can set him straight about why you need his information."

Wanda glanced over at the counter in the kitchen where their food was sitting and the manager was still glowering. Wanda slipped out of the booth, grabbed the food, and slid it in front of them. Myrtle smiled at her.

Emily didn't seem to register that Wanda had just done her job. She continued, sounding troubled, "You know, it wasn't like Hortense was really all that awful. She had her good traits, like everybody does. I didn't have any hard feelings against her."

Myrtle swallowed down a bite of her lumberjack breakfast. "Didn't you, dear? That's very good of you."

Emily shrugged. "When it all happened, I think I was too stunned to even make a fuss. It was like I'd dreamed our whole conversation. Then later, I figured maybe I'd misunderstood everything. When Hortense went ballistic on me in her yard, I didn't argue or anything. I told her I'd replant the Hosta and the fern I'd divided, but she wanted me out of her yard immediately. I mean, in her eyes, she thought I was a thief. I get that she just wanted me gone."

Wanda had been chewing her food thoughtfully. Then she said, "You really love them plants."

Emily grinned at her. "It's pretty obvious, isn't it? Yeah, I've always loved plants and gardening." She paused, thinking. "I was one of those offbeat kids in school. I never had a lot of friends, but it didn't bother me because I felt so much at home out in nature. That's where I was accepted. I wanted to be a horticulturist, but I don't have the money for school."

"Your parents couldn't help?" asked Myrtle delicately. She had the feeling she remembered something about Emily's parents, but she wasn't positive.

Emily shook her head. "They died in a car accident a couple of years ago."

Everyone at the booth gave her a sad look. Myrtle said, "I'm very sorry to hear that, dear."

"It's okay. I've gotten used to it now, although it was a total shock at the time. But even before they died, they weren't going to send me to school, either. Both of them worked so hard, but never had much money. They rented an apartment, too, so there wasn't any land for them to pass along." Emily shrugged. "It's just the way it is."

Myrtle glanced over at the diner manager, who was getting increasingly agitated about their long visit with Emily. No new customers had entered the diner, though, and the other waitress seemed to handle the tables that Emily had been taking care of. Myrtle had one more important question to ask Emily.

"Do you know of anybody else that Hortense wasn't getting along with? Can you think of somebody who might have wanted to murder her? Because if the police have a more likely suspect, they might focus on you less," said Myrtle.

Emily brightened at this. "That's true." Then her face clouded. "I don't like putting suspicion on anybody, though."

"You're just helping us figure out who did this terrible thing to Hortense," said Myrtle evenly.

"So you'll pass the information on to Red?"

Myrtle gave her a rather insincere smile. "Of course, dear."

Emily took a deep breath. "Well, I hate to say this, but Martha Green. She'd been really sweet to me after the Hortense incident. She told me that Hortense didn't have good communication skills or interpersonal skills. Martha reminded me how passionate and possessive of her plants Hortense was."

Myrtle arched her brow. "And that made you feel kindlier toward Hortense?"

"Sure, it did. Martha said that Hortense hadn't been raised right, which was pretty obvious once she pointed it out."

Miles murmured, "It sounds like Martha was being very diplomatic and understanding of Hortense's behavior."

"Yes, she was," said Emily. "But then, right after that, she started being very critical of Hortense. She couldn't believe Hortense was picked to be the grand judge at the flower show. She thought Hortense was the worst possible choice, even though she was so knowledgeable about plants. Martha thought people were going to be leaving the flower show in tears while Hortense gloated."

Wanda, having quickly cleaned her plate, listened to Emily with interest.

Emily continued, "She said Hortense had terrible manners, no empathy, and was completely egotistical. I was a little confused at Martha's total turnaround in what she was saying about Hortense. Martha could tell I couldn't figure out what to make of it, so she told me she'd had an incident with Hortense recently, herself."

"What was the incident?" asked Myrtle.

"She didn't say too much else about it. Martha kind of reeled herself back in. What I gathered, though, is that Martha is a total perfectionist. Did you see her entry in the arrangement exhibit?"

Myrtle thought back to the rather odd photo and nodded. It hadn't been to Myrtle's taste, but the elaborate arrangement had certainly been eye-catching. And, she supposed, perfectly constructed.

Emily continued, "Martha thought Hortense was jealous of Martha's natural ability and her popularity and set out to sabotage her somehow. But Martha didn't give any details. And I'm not saying that Martha had anything to do with Hortense's death," she added in a rush. "She was so sweet to me after I had that run-in with Hortense."

The manager had finally lost patience and was heading their way. Myrtle quickly said, "I'm afraid you're about to have another run-in, dear."

Emily looked up and said, "Oh!"

The manager's face was red as he jerked his thumb to indicate that Emily needed to get back to work. She leaped up from the booth, apologizing.

Myrtle hopped in smoothly. "It was all my fault, sir. I needed to talk with Emily about an important matter. It wasn't a social visit."

The manager seemed somewhat less agitated than he'd been previously. He gave Myrtle a curt nod, then took away their empty plates since Emily had hurried off without doing so. Then he put the check down on the table.

Miles picked up the check. "I think it's time for us to leave," he said to Myrtle and Wanda.

"Yep," said Wanda. "Think they're about done with us today."

Miles paid up while Myrtle and Wanda finished their coffees. Then they headed for the door. When they reached Miles's car, Myrtle saw Lieutenant Perkins from the state police walking toward the door of the diner.

"Lt. Perkins," she sang out.

Perkins smiled at her and headed over. "How are you, Miss Myrtle? Mr. Bradford? And . . . Wanda, isn't it? I'm sorry, I don't know your last name."

"Jest Wanda," said Wanda shyly.

"Good to see you, Perkins, even if it's under these horrible circumstances," said Myrtle.

Perkins said, "It usually is under pretty grim circumstances, isn't it? I'll have to come by some other time just to catch up with you. How are things going when you're not discovering bodies? You're feeling well?"

"Never better," assured Myrtle. "How's your dear mother?"

Perkins said, "Still knocking out those crossword puzzles. I'm going to introduce her to chess, soon. Or *re*introduce her to it. She said she used to play when she was a young teen, but that's been a while."

Miles pushed his glasses up his nose, looking interested. "It's a great game."

"Miles is quite a chess player himself," said Myrtle. She smiled at Perkins. "On quite a different topic, I don't suppose you could share some information about Hortense's death? Such a terrible thing to happen at the flower show, isn't it? Wanda and I were quite startled to find her there when we'd been expecting to view a horticultural exhibit. Anyway, if you could simply provide me information with the sorts of things I wouldn't know. Was there physical evidence collected?"

Perkins remained just as deferential, even though Myrtle was pumping him for information. "There was some physical evidence collected, yes."

Myrtle raised her eyebrows. "The sort of physical evidence that may immediately point to the killer and wrap up the case?"

Perkins shook his head. "That would be preferred, of course, but the physical evidence that was collected doesn't match anyone in our database. And we can't go around Bradley taking clothing samples or fingerprints."

"No, I suppose not." Myrtle sounded delighted by this news instead of disappointed. It meant that she could continue investigating and perhaps beat Red to the punch again.

Perkins smiled at her. "I don't suppose *you* have any information you'd like to share, Mrs. Clover? I know you're particularly gifted at this sort of thing."

Myrtle puffed up with pride. "I guess I'm a gifted amateur. But no, I don't really have anything to share."

Miles stared pointedly at the diner, where they'd had a quite recent interesting conversation with Emily. Myrtle ignored him.

Perkins said, "Got it. Well, I hope the three of you have a much-better day than you've had so far. I'm picking up lunch for the team, so I'd better head inside."

They said their goodbyes and then hopped into Miles's car.

"Shouldn't you have told Perkins about Emily? He provided you with information, after all," said Miles.

"Only in the very *vaguest* of ways. Yes, they have physical evidence. No, it doesn't currently help them. But it's good that, when we solve the case, they'll have evidence on hand that can help convict the killer."

Miles said with a touch of censure in his voice, "Then shouldn't you have given *Perkins* information in the very vaguest of ways? Just to be fair and square?"

Myrtle sniffed. "But it's not fair and square at all, is it? It's just the three of us against a local police department and the state police. They have tons of resources. I'm on a strict budget until my check comes at the beginning of the month. Since it's not intrinsically fair, I have to level the playing field."

Miles sighed. "I suppose you're right. I don't mind not sharing information with Red, but Perkins is a lot friendlier. It feels as if we should help him out in our joint goal of finding the killer." He paused. "What are we all doing now? Heading over to Myrtle's house?"

Wanda cleared her throat from the backseat and carefully said, "I got Dan pickin' me up from Myrtle's."

"Pooh," said Myrtle. "I was hoping we could have a rousing game of hearts. Has he already set out, do you think?"

Wanda drawled, "I got the feelin' he's already there."

Sure enough, Dan's vehicle, blowing out noxious-smelling fumes, was idling in front of Myrtle's house when they pulled up. Dan was looking rather impatient.

Myrtle said, "I'm glad you were with me today, Wanda. It was quite unsettling, wasn't it? Are you fully recovered from it all now?"

Because Wanda did indeed look tired. But she nodded and gave her winning gap-toothed grin. "I'm good. Thanks fer lunch, Miles."

She hesitated for a moment. "Been seein' weird visions lately," muttered Wanda.

"Have you?" asked Myrtle with a frown. "Your visions have always seemed very matter-of-fact, except during those times when the Sight is being inscrutable. Your horoscopes warn people to water their new shrub or to get their oil changed."

Wanda nodded. "Yeah. Kinda odd."

"Are the visions about any particular person?" asked Miles.

"Yep. About Dan."

Myrtle said, "Well, if they're visions about your brother, I can understand them being weird. Crazy Dan isn't exactly the most ordinary of people. What kinds of things are you seeing?"

"Jest stuff like him drinkin' coffee in some kitchen."

"Not your kitchen?" asked Miles.

Wanda shook her head. "Some other kitchen." She paused. "Dan don't drink coffee."

"That is rather mysterious," agreed Myrtle. "Do you think it could signify something?"

"If it does, I sure don't git it."

Myrtle noticed that her friend was looking rather anxious. Although Crazy Dan seemed to bother Wanda quite a bit with his reckless spending, his messiness, and his overall impetuous and noisy personality, she knew Wanda always felt a sense of responsibility toward her brother. She asked briskly, "Dan doesn't appear to be in any danger in these visions?"

Wanda considered this. Then she shook her head.

"He seems comfortable? Happy, even?"

Wanda nodded. "Jest sorta weird."

"It definitely is. But since your brother appears to be safe in these visions, I'm thinking they're not worth worrying over. Have you told Dan about them?"

Another quick shake of her head. "Nope. Dan don't understand how the Sight works."

"I'm certain he doesn't. I'd just keep it all to myself. But the important thing is not to worry, Wanda."

Miles nodded. "It could be that the vision is a sign of good things to come."

"I reckon so," said Wanda, looking more cheerful.

Miles reached into his pocket and pulled out a wad of bills, pressing it quickly into Wanda's hand before she stepped out of the car. And before Dan could see and appropriate the money for his out-of-control online shopping habit.

"Thanks," said Wanda again. Then she was whisked away by her brother in a cloud of exhaust.

Chapter Five

Myrtle said, "We could watch *Tomorrow's Promise*. I want to find out more about Octavia's evil twin resurfacing."

Miles followed her into the house. "The show had retired that evil twin storyline before I started watching the show with you. What was the background there?"

"Ohhhh, it's a lot. Octavia's evil twin is Vivienne Montague. Octavia has always been portrayed as this saintly character who has so much to put up with. Vivienne mowed down their parents with their own car, killing them both, to inherit their vast fortune. The kicker is that Vivienne was only ten years old at the time."

Miles frowned. "Could the kid even see over the steering wheel?"

"She's very tall. And now she's back."

Miles added, "I suppose she's claiming she suffered amnesia."

"Correct. And she says she's turned over a new leaf. But she *clearly* hasn't, because what fun would that be? I'm sure she has plans to steal Octavia's husband."

Myrtle's phone rang. "Fiddlesticks. Who's calling right when *Tomorrow's Promise* is about to come on?"

It was Elaine, Red's wife, and Myrtle's daughter-in-law. "Myrtle?" asked a pitiful voice on the other end of the line.

"Elaine? Whatever's happened? You sound dreadful." And then, as an even worse thought crossed Myrtle's mind, she demanded, "Is Jack okay?"

"Yes, Jack's fine. But I've done something ridiculous to my neck when I was doing a headstand for yoga."

Myrtle decided to overlook the fact that Elaine had no business standing on her head, despite the fact she was only in her thirties. "What can I do to help? Take you to the doctor? The emergency room?"

"Oh, I actually did a virtual visit with the doctor, so I'm good. She prescribed a muscle relaxer and a steroid. She thinks it's a bad pull. The only problem is that I can't drive my car like this; I can barely turn my head. I need to get to the pharmacy to pick up the prescriptions. Do you think you can come over and drive me there? In my car?"

Myrtle said, "Of *course* I can. Mercy. Or I can pick it up myself and bring it to you."

"I appreciate it, but I did promise Jack that he could come with me. He was sad that I had a boo-boo, and the pharmacy has a jar of lollipops for children. Is it all right if he and I both come along with you?"

"Certainly! It'll be an adventure." Myrtle hung up the phone.

Miles said, "Do you need me to drive you somewhere?"

Myrtle quickly filled him in. Miles said, "So I can drive all of you."

"You don't have a child seat, so that plan won't work. And you're not used to driving a minivan, so you shouldn't drive Elaine's."

Miles tilted his head to one side. "Are *you* used to driving a minivan?"

"No, but I'm extremely adaptable. Anyway, *Tomorrow's Promise* is taping, so we can watch it later. Sorry to ditch on our plans."

Miles said, "I'm sure the show and all its shenanigans can wait a bit for us." He walked toward the door. "See you later, Myrtle."

Myrtle grabbed her purse and headed across the street to Elaine's house. Elaine was already standing gingerly in the driveway with Jack. Jack's face split into a huge grin when he saw Myrtle walking up. "Nana!" he called out. He hugged her legs.

Myrtle beamed at him. "Who's the best boy ever?"

"Jack!"

They grinned at each other in total agreement.

Elaine said ruefully, "I saw Miles leaving your house. I'm sorry about interrupting your visit. And it occurs to me that it's time for your soap opera, too."

"Pish! As if I'd want to watch a silly soap opera instead of spending time with you two." Myrtle took the keys from Elaine. "Now, do we need to do anything to make you feel more comfortable in the front seat, Elaine? A pillow? An ice pack?"

Elaine shook her head and then winced at the movement. "No, I think that medicine is the only thing that's really going to take the edge off."

Myrtle slid open the minivan door and said, "Jack? Can you be a big boy and climb into your seat?"

As Myrtle expected, Jack did precisely what he was told. What was more, he even buckled himself in. Then he grinned at Myrtle, who clapped for him. Elaine carefully eased into the passenger seat.

Myrtle said, "Now, let me adjust my mirrors and get acquainted with the controls." She was glad she took a minute, because the dashboard looked like something out of an airplane cockpit. She finally decided that she wouldn't need anything but the steering wheel, brake, and accelerator. They set off at a sedate fifteen miles an hour.

Jack started singing "Old MacDonald Had a Farm," and soon Elaine and Myrtle were clucking, oinking, and neighing along with him as Myrtle creeped down the street toward downtown and the pharmacy. Once they reached downtown, they saw Red standing outside the police station. He stared in shock as the minivan slowly approached. Myrtle gave a merry toot of the horn and a jaunty wave. Red looked horrified to see his wife and child in the vehicle along with her. He jumped into his police cruiser and followed them.

Elaine sighed. "I did leave a message with Red to let him know about my injury. But it seems like he's been too busy to see his messages."

A few minutes later, Myrtle pulled carefully into the pharmacy. She was aggravated to see Red drive into the parking lot behind her. "I was going to head for the drive-through window, but he clearly wants to have a word," she said between gritted teeth.

Elaine sighed. "I suppose you should park for a moment before we go to the drive-through. Otherwise, he'll turn on his lights and siren."

Jack clapped his hands, thinking that sounded like the best thing ever.

Myrtle coasted into a parking spot and, after taking a few seconds to ascertain where the button was, rolled down her window. Red hopped out of his police cruiser. "This needs to be brief, Red. Your wife is in severe discomfort and needs her medicine."

"What? She was just fine when I left this morning." Red gave his mother a suspicious look, as if she'd somehow managed to harm Elaine before hijacking her vehicle.

Elaine said, "I pulled something in my neck when I was doing yoga."

Understanding now swept across Red's features, and he nodded. Elaine's hobbies rarely went well, and it was to be expected that yoga, the gentlest of hobbies, would end poorly. "Are you okay? Do you need to go to the doctor?"

Myrtle made an irritated sound. "I've already asked her that, Red. She's had a virtual visit, and we're picking up her medication and a lollipop for Jack now."

Red muttered, "Y'all could have walked here quicker."

"What was that?" asked Myrtle, frowning.

"I just said I'd give y'all a police escort on your way home. Then I need to get back to the station."

Myrtle wanted to ask Red how the investigation was going so far. Particularly which suspects he'd been speaking with. But she wanted to get Elaine her muscle relaxer and steroid, so she merely bobbed her head at her son, rolled up the window, and headed for the drive-through window. A couple of minutes later, they were making their way out of the parking lot with Red at the helm. He turned on his blue lights, which made Jack cheer and wave his lollipop in the air. At least Red hadn't turned his siren on. Cars slowed down and got out of the way as soon as their small, slow-moving motorcade approached.

"I'm glad you called me, Elaine. You know I can always help whenever you need me," said Myrtle.

Elaine smiled at her. "Well, I didn't want to bother you. Like I said, I tried calling Red first. Saturdays are usually a pretty quiet day for him at work. Until Saturday night rolls around, of course. Then there's usually mayhem over at the bar that Red has to attend to. But he didn't answer his phone." She shrugged.

Myrtle said, "Oh gracious, you've been so busy with your virtual visit and your injury that you hadn't even heard the news."

"What news?" asked Elaine curiously.

Myrtle didn't really want to talk about murder in front of an impressionable two-year-old, but fortunately Jack started to give them a loud rendition of "Baa-Baa Black Sheep" right then so Myrtle could quickly fill in Elaine.

"At the flower show! That's just insane. What kind of crazy person murders someone with that many people around?" asked Elaine.

"A desperate person. Someone who needs Hortense out of the way quickly. Or perhaps someone who lost their temper with Hortense. Did you know her?"

Elaine shrugged. "Not particularly well. Just through the garden club. She always seemed sort of prickly to me. And you know how it is when I take Jack over to the Piggly Wiggly to get groceries."

"You mean how everyone fawns over him, telling you he's so adorable and should be in commercials?" asked Myrtle. The last bit might have been Myrtle exaggerating. But Myrtle felt strongly that Jack should be in commercials.

"That's right. When I saw Hortense at the Piggly Wiggly, she shrank back as if she might catch cooties from Jack."

Myrtle pressed her lips together. That right there told her all she needed to know about Hortense. Shrinking back from her precious grandbaby, *indeed*. While she was fuming over that, she noticed out the window that Earl Jenkins, Hortense's fired landscaper, was sitting on a park bench, feeding birds. She had the feeling she'd soon be heading in that direction herself.

They were soon at Red and Elaine's house. Red looked grimly pleased that they'd made it safely home. He gave them a curt wave and quickly headed back downtown.

Myrtle made sure Elaine was settled comfortably inside with her medication, a glass of water, and a heating pad. She wasn't at all sure the heating pad was needed, but it was much more pleasant than ice. Then she put on Jack's favorite cartoon to keep him quiet and busy, told Elaine she'd check on her later, and slipped out the door.

Soon Myrtle was walking with determination toward the park. If Earl Jenkins had recently been fired by Hortense, then he certainly had a bone to pick with her. Perhaps he hadn't been able to restrain himself and had slung the flowerpot at Hortense's head. The fact he was feeding birds at the park made it seem as if he had more free time on his hands than usual. Myrtle couldn't recall Earl doing such a thing before. Ordinarily, he was out maintaining the nicest yards in town.

A few minutes into her walk, Pasha joined her, smiling her feline smile up at Myrtle.

"Pasha! My brilliant darling. Are you accompanying me to the park?"

Pasha gave a definitive mew.

"How very perceptive of you. We'll be visiting a man who's feeding birds. You're not planning on subduing nature again, are you?"

Pasha blinked innocently at Myrtle, still smiling enigmatically.

"Then let's go find Mr. Jenkins. I do believe he'll have items of interest to share with us."

Pasha, being a most remarkable animal, loped alongside Myrtle as she walked down the sidewalk. Myrtle's cane thumped emphatically as she went. Shortly, they made it to the park. Myrtle was relieved to see that Earl Jenkins was still a fixture on the park bench. He appeared to be done feeding the birds and was now surveying one of the park's shrubs with evident displeasure on his face. He was a grizzled, middle-aged man with rough-hewn features and a weathered countenance.

"Hello there," said Myrtle brightly. "Do you mind if I sit next to you on the bench? I do believe the walk from my house took a bit more out of me than I expected. I'm somewhat winded."

He obligingly scooted over to the side, giving a curious look at Pasha, who settled quietly next to Myrtle's feet. "Good day to you, Miss Myrtle. How are things going in your neck of the woods?"

For a moment, Myrtle thought of Emily telling her that a man at the park could provide her with an alibi, if only he could be tracked down. She flittingly wondered if Earl could be that man, but then dismissed the idea, since Emily had plainly said it was a young man. Emily was the age that she likely considered anyone over the age of thirty to be old.

"Oh, everything in my neck of the woods has been rather busy, Earl. But that keeps us young, doesn't it?"

He gave her a doubtful look, but smiled politely. "I suppose it does, Miss Myrtle." He paused. "I heard that your morning was especially hectic. Word has it you were the one who discovered Hortense Winston today."

Chapter Six

"I'm afraid so. Such a tragedy, isn't it? You were at the flower show yourself this morning, weren't you? I believe I spotted you making the rounds."

Earl stiffened. "I was there," he said warily. "Viewing the different exhibits and whatnot."

"Were you in the audience for the opening remarks? I'd imagine you'd have wanted to be there to hear Hortense announce the winners of the different categories."

"Pah," said Earl. "I don't enjoy listening to speeches, and I don't much care for anyone's opinion but my own. I could make up my own mind as to the various exhibits and who was a worthy winner. I didn't need Hortense Winston to parse it out for me." He glanced at Myrtle. "As I recall, you had a stunner of a rose in last year's flower show. It should have won, for sure."

Myrtle beamed at him. "You're so perceptive, Earl! I did indeed have a lovely rosebush. Sadly, this year it was ravished by deer."

"That's very unfortunate."

"Indeed it is," said Myrtle darkly. "My next-door neighbor has been feeding the things. It's most upsetting." She paused.

"So I understand you didn't think much of Hortense being the grand judge? Wasn't there something of a contretemps between the two of you lately? You do know how the gossips are in Bradley."

Earl sighed. "I knew that story was making the rounds. Hortense was spreading it everywhere. I've no doubt your son will be speaking with me soon about it."

"But he hasn't yet?"

"No," said Earl.

Myrtle beamed once again. She dearly loved being ahead of the curve, especially when it came to Red.

"It would certainly help if you had an alibi, Earl. I'm sure Red wouldn't be able to make much of a suspect out of you if you did."

Earl shook his head. "I'm afraid that's out of the question. I usually go to these kinds of things solo, and I did today. There was nobody to confirm where I was before you discovered Hortense's body."

"You were in and out of the exhibits?" asked Myrtle.

He nodded.

"And yet you didn't see Hortense?"

Earl said, "I was spending a good deal of time in the rose room. Figured I'd have the chance to see what was there before the auditorium emptied and the rooms were swarmed. There was a bench in there, and I took a seat and took my time looking at them."

"But you didn't hear any indications of violence coming from the horticulture division?"

Earl glanced down at Pasha, who was blinking steadily at him. He said, "No, I didn't. It's become my habit when I'm working to listen to podcasts of different sorts. I had my Bluetooth earbuds in and was listening away. World War III could have started up down the hall, and I'd never have heard a thing."

"That's a pity," said Myrtle. She looked over at Earl, who was still looking warily at Pasha. "I believe Pasha would like you to feed the birds again."

A look of relief passed over Earl's features. "Oh, is that it? She looked as if she wanted to eat me alive."

"No, she'd like to eat the birds alive. And have you act as her accessory to the crime."

Earl smiled down at Pasha. "Sorry, kitty. The birdseed is all gone. And so are the birds, now that you're here."

Pasha swished her tail in irritation. Finding Earl no longer interesting, she stalked off to try her luck in a different section of the park.

While Earl was distracted by Pasha's grand exit, Myrtle took the opportunity to ask a tougher question. "Tell me why Hortense fired you."

Earl raised his eyebrows. "I thought everybody already knew about that."

"What people think they know and what they actually know are frequently not the same thing. I'd rather hear it from you."

Earl said, "Fair enough. First off, no matter what Hortense might have said, she did not fire me. I quit. I was tired of the way she treated me. She acted like I had no idea what I was doing in her garden. But I've been caring for plants my whole life. I've always been really respected, you know?"

"I've always heard you're the best yardman in town, Earl. It's just a pity I can't afford you. That's why I'm stuck with Dusty."

Earl gave a crooked smile. "Ahh, Dusty. Dusty knows a lot about yards, too."

"He knows a lot about not showing up for work," said Myrtle sourly.

"Maybe he does. I remember one time, Dusty's gas-powered mower was broken. He tried to fix it himself to save money."

Myrtle snorted. "I don't think Dusty is particularly handy."

"No, maybe not. Anyway, I was taking care of a yard directly across the street from one Dusty was working on. I spotted Dusty out there with some kind of old-fashioned push mower . . . one of those reel mowers."

Myrtle nodded. "I remember those from when I was a little girl."

"They'll do the job, of course, but it'll take the whole day. Dusty must have gotten impatient, because he threw the thing down while I was watching. He grabbed a weed whacker off his truck, but got tangled up in an extension cord in the truck bed and fell over." Earl shook his head, chuckling. "He's just the victim of his own bad luck."

"The victim of his own profound laziness, more like."

Earl smiled. "That probably doesn't help, either." He paused, and they sat quietly on the bench, listening to the sounds of birds in the trees. Earl said slowly, "Because I spent so much time around Hortense, working with her, I can say that her personal life was a mess."

"Divorced, wasn't she? I thought I recalled she was married to Harold Daniels."

"That's right—the guy who owns the hardware store. Their relationship didn't work out, though, so she left him. She's been dating another guy, Arthur Wilkins. Do you know him?"

Myrtle said, "He's one of the botanists, isn't he? The one that isn't Ezra. Arthur has spoken at my garden club meetings. I'm acquainted with him. I didn't realize the two of them were dating."

"Well, they're not dating anymore. He's been in a huff because Hortense dumped him. Apparently, she insulted him, to boot."

Myrtle nodded. "So you think both Harold and Arthur have reason to be upset with Hortense."

"Exactly. I'm not saying they'd be upset enough to murder her, but you just never know, do you? Harold is the kind of guy who just plays it off in public, acting like he doesn't care that his wife left him. But deep down, I could tell he was furious. He's not the sort of person who's used to being dumped. Arthur was different—just kind of icy about it. Neither one of those guys was happy with her." Earl shrugged. "Of course, the cops will say that *I* wasn't happy with her, either. And I wasn't. But I didn't want her to die."

"You were going to tell me what actually happened that day in Hortense's yard," prompted Myrtle.

Earl sighed. "Believe me, I'm just sick about it. I love living things. And I've always done a great job helping Hortense with her yard. I didn't just go out there to mow, you know. I was in charge of weeding and pruning, too. Hortense always said I did a great job making her garden look its best. The last thing I want to do is to harm anybody's plants and flowers. It was just a stupid, stupid mistake. I had a lot on my mind that day. The problem with owning your own business is that you're a one-man band. I was trying to think of a way I could wrangle just one week off. I felt like I needed something of a break."

"You were distracted and made an error? It's happened to all of us."

Earl shook his head. "Well, it sure hadn't happened to me. Not like this. I picked up my sprayer, thinking it was the one with fertilizer in it. But it was the one that had weedkiller in it, instead. I killed those prize roses just as if I'd put a gun to their heads. Didn't even realize it until much later that day."

Myrtle said, "And Hortense, who's not the most patient or forgiving person in the world, gave you a hard time over it."

Earl snorted. "That's a nice way of putting it. Hortense was furious. But she didn't fire me. She decided, instead, to tell everybody in town about what happened. I mean, this is my livelihood. I've been working in this field for a couple of decades, and I've never done anything remotely this bad before. Of all the people in the world, I had to screw up at Hortense's house."

"And you quit."

"Sure. I couldn't handle her haranguing me all the time. I was polite about it. I told her I thought she'd do better with a different yard guy. Then Hortense flipped the script and said that she'd fired me." Earl shrugged. "I couldn't win. And here I am on a park bench, feeding the birds. How the mighty have fallen," he said ruefully. "Hortense made sure I had plenty of free time by spreading the story."

Earl was quiet for a few moments, taking in the scene. Myrtle did the same. There were two dog-walkers who were allowing their furry offspring to greet each other. The golden retriever was grinning a huge doggy grin as his tail wagged wildly, while the Shetland Sheepdog had an imperious expression on her face and appeared to be looking down her long nose at the golden. Farther away, a young couple lounged on a checkered blanket beneath the shade of a tremendous old oak tree. They were laughing and sharing a meal of sandwiches.

Earl said, "I haven't lived here as long as you have, Miss Myrtle. But it's always been home to me."

The sound of regret in his voice made Myrtle turn to look at him. "It sounds as if you're planning on making your goodbyes to Bradley."

He nodded. "At first, it was just something I was kicking around in my brain. Jobs are pretty limited here, you know."

"Well, there are only so many people who live here. Looking at it from your standpoint, there's a limited pool of potential candidates for your landscaping services. Not everyone can afford to have you take care of your yard. Which is why, as we mentioned before, I'm stuck with Dusty."

Earl said, "Right. So we've got the limited pool. Then that pool got tainted."

Myrtle pursed her lips. "Well, I hate to think all your customers are going to turn on you. Hortense might have been poisonous, but let's face it—the pool of potential landscaping *businesses* is also limited. The choices are Dusty, Tiny, yourself, and maybe one or two others. Maybe your customers might just have to grit their teeth and bear it."

"Right. Except I don't like that. Not at all. I feel like I spent most of my life here building this great reputation for myself."

They were both quiet again, looking out into the park. The young couple now appeared to be toasting each other with beverages in tumblers. Earl looked glumly at them, perhaps feeling more down when seeing people so very happy.

Earl finally continued. "I don't like the idea of my customers gritting their teeth and bearing it. I want them to be excited when I come over and take care of their property and make it look its best. I don't like the looks they're giving me, thinking I'm going to squirt weedkiller on their prized plants. And I don't like the gossip that's going on. I think my time in Bradley is over, Miss Myrtle."

She nodded. "Well, I can certainly understand that. There've been plenty of times when I've been quite irritated with the town of Bradley. And times I've been bored here, too."

Earl gave her a grin. "I guess that's when you start causing trouble. I've seen those gnomes in your yard many times."

"Yes, those are there to warn Red not to get involved in my business, even when I'm causing trouble. *Especially* when I'm causing trouble."

Earl said, "I liked that pirate gnome that I saw in your yard last time."

Myrtle beamed at him. "Isn't he handsome? Such a little swashbuckler with his eyepatch, tricorn hat, and miniature pirate ship." She paused. "If you move from Bradley, where might you go?"

Earl had a wistful look on his face. "When I was in my twenties, I always thought it would be great to work for the botanical gardens near Charlotte."

"The Daniel Stowe gardens? I've heard those are lovely."

Earl said eagerly, "They are. They have a conservatory with tropical plants and orchids that's amazing. They have a small cottage garden, a canal garden, and walking trails. They even have a children's garden there."

"You never interviewed there?"

Earl's smile faded away. "I did, actually. But I didn't make it."

"But you were in your twenties, you were saying. You likely didn't have the expertise they were looking for at the time. Now you're on the other side. You've had experience and years of successfully managing plants."

Earl looked ruefully at her. "Maybe I should have you write my cover letter."

"I'd be happy to. If you're interested in a job there, you're certainly well-qualified to get one."

"Thanks, Miss Myrtle. I'll let you know. Maybe I can try to use some of my contacts, too. That might help me get a leg in."

"Networking is always a great way to get employment," agreed Myrtle.

Earl stretched and then stood up. "I guess I'd better be on my way. I have another yard to tackle soon. At least I didn't lose all my business."

"See you, Earl," said Myrtle absently as he walked toward the parking lot and his truck.

Myrtle sat in the park for several more minutes, turning everything over in her head. Then she texted Elaine to see how she was doing. Elaine said that she was as comfortable as she could be, under the circumstances. Myrtle could hear the happy sounds of Jack's cartoon in the background and was glad he was still entertained.

Myrtle rose from the bench and glanced around to see if Pasha wanted to go back with her. But Pasha was hunting, crouched under a low-hanging bush, and gave Myrtle an apologetic look. "You enjoy, darling girl," said Myrtle.

She walked back home, her cane thumping on the sidewalk as she went. Halfway home, she saw an ancient Buick that she recognized as belonging to Priscilla Abrams, who was also ancient. As she recalled, Priscilla lived next door to Hortense. She wondered what Priscilla's impression of Hortense had been. Myrtle attempted to look very frail and withered, despite her big bones and healthy glow. Her ruse worked, and Priscilla pulled over immediately, looking at Myrtle with concern.

"Gracious, Myrtle! Are you all right? You look tuckered out."

Myrtle gave her a piteous look. "Priscilla? Is that you? I haven't seen you for an age."

"Are you on your way back home? I can drive you there." Priscilla's face was wrought with concern.

"Could you, my dear?" asked Myrtle in a faint voice. "That would be most kind of you. Especially since you seem to be heading in the opposite direction."

Priscilla waved her hand to indicate the direction she was previously traveling in had no relation to anything at all. "It would be my pleasure. Hop in."

With that, Myrtle opened the door of the ancient Buick and climbed in. Sadly, Priscilla seemed much more concerned with diagnosing and treating Myrtle's mysterious ailment than she did with talking about Hortense.

"You might be dehydrated. I was dehydrated just last year, and it was a terrible thing. I was simply determined to get my yardwork done, but it was the hottest day of the year. I didn't do a good job drinking water. The next thing I knew, I was terribly weak! I had to get an IV bag at the hospital. Do you think I should take you to the hospital?" Prisilla's face was lined with worry.

"No, dear. I have lots of water at home. You're right about the water, though. I haven't been drinking it as I should."

Priscilla said, "I know. I'll call Red. He'll know what to do."

Myrtle's eyes opened wide with alarm. "Let's not call Red. He's terribly busy right now, you know. With Hortense's murder."

Now it was Priscilla's turn to open her eyes wide. "Gracious, I forgot! Such a terrible thing. You know Hortense lived right next door to me." She frowned. "Did I hear you were the one who found her? You and the psychic lady?"

"Wanda, yes. Unfortunately, we did."

Priscilla said, "What a terrible thing! I tell you, sometimes I lie awake at night and worry about what the world is coming to. What on earth happened?"

Myrtle gave Priscilla a quick and undetailed overview of that morning as Priscilla pulled into Myrtle's driveway.

"Such evil. I simply cannot imagine."

Myrtle said, "I know. It's hard to wrap one's head around. I'll be writing an article about this for the *Bradley Bugle*, and I hope that will help me digest what happened. Since you were so close to Hortense, do you have any insight as to whom might be upset with her?"

"Oh, I wouldn't say I was *close* to Hortense."

Myrtle said, "*Physically*, close. Next door." Myrtle bit back a sigh. Priscilla had never been the sharpest tool in the shed.

"I see. Well, you know, I think people have always been jealous of her lovely garden. I do have to work especially hard on my yard just to make sure it doesn't look positively hideous next to Hortense's." She gave Myrtle an expectant look, as if waiting for Myrtle to tell her that was wonderful insight.

But Myrtle wanted a bit more information than that. "Yes, but I wouldn't say any of those people would murder Hortense because of yard envy, would you?"

Priscilla flushed. "No, you're probably right." She thought hard. Then she brightened. "There is that poor girl. Emily, I think her name is. Hortense made her most upset."

"Was that the day Emily tried to take some plants from her yard?"

Priscilla nodded eagerly. "The same day. I didn't know what was going on. Hortense lived by herself currently, of course, yet I could hear loud noises coming from her backyard. I went outside to make sure Hortense wasn't being attacked by some scoundrel or something. But then I heard Emily and Hortense arguing."

"You know Emily?"

Priscilla said, "Only as my waitress at the diner. She tries hard, doesn't she?"

She didn't seem to try hard enough as far as Myrtle could see.

"Anyway," continued Priscilla. "Emily was yelling at Hortense. I was terribly surprised. She's always such a pleasant young woman when she's at the diner."

Emily had said that she hadn't had an angry exchange with Hortense. Myrtle said, "Could you hear what Emily was saying?"

Priscilla hesitated. "I wouldn't want you to think I was eavesdropping."

"Of course I wouldn't." Although Myrtle suspected Priscilla's life was such that eavesdropping on an exciting conversation wouldn't be completely out of character.

"I couldn't help but overhear, since Emily's voice was raised. She was telling Hortense that she'd asked her for the Hosta and the giant fern. That Hortense had agreed to let Emily divide them and plant them in her own yard."

Myrtle said, "And Hortense disagreed with Emily?"

"I'm afraid Hortense was very upset with the poor young woman. Perhaps it was some sort of misunderstanding? At any rate, I heard Hortense threaten to call Red and report Emily for trespassing and theft." Priscilla's big eyes were clouded with worry at the memory.

"That seems very petty of Hortense. But then, it seems she'd been on a tear of pettiness recently. I understand she let Earl, her yardman, go."

Priscilla said, "Isn't that such a shame? He's such an amazing landscaper. If I had the money, I'd love to hire him to help in my yard."

"Me, too. You didn't overhear Hortense's exchange with Earl by any chance, did you?"

Priscilla gave her a reproachful look. "No, of course not. I don't make a habit of eavesdropping, you know."

Myrtle said, "Naturally, dear. I guess it was just wishful thinking. Like I was saying, I wanted to get a little background on this story I'm writing for the paper."

"You won't put my name on any quotations, will you?" Priscilla looked alarmed.

"No, I wouldn't dream of it. Thanks so much for running me home. I'd better head inside and get started with my water."

Priscilla called out after her, "And sports drinks, if you have them! Those electrolytes are so very important."

Myrtle smiled and waved. Then she walked away from Priscilla and toward her front door with relief. That was quite enough visiting for one day. Aside from writing the article for Sloan Jones, her editor, she had no plans for the remainder of the day.

She immediately called Sloan at the *Bradley Bugle* office to let him know.

"*Bradley Bugle*," answered Sloan, absently.

"It's Myrtle Clover, Sloan."

Sloan suddenly sounded a lot more alert as he said, "Miss Myrtle!"

Myrtle's lips curved. Sloan always sounded just like he had in high school when he hadn't brought in his homework or was caught flying paper airplanes in class. "Hi there, Sloan. I just wanted to let you know you needed to save some room on the front page of tomorrow's paper for me."

"The Sunday edition?" Sloan sounded troubled, as well he might. The Sunday paper was the best-selling edition of the week. Folks who didn't subscribe to the paper usually picked it up at the Piggly Wiggly on Sundays.

"The very one. I happened to discover poor Hortense Winston this morning." Although Myrtle was rapidly getting the impression poor Hortense wasn't a particularly kind person.

Now Sloan sounded even more troubled. "I see." He hesitated. "I was going to call you, Miss Myrtle. I'd like you to have a much more interesting assignment than covering Hortense's death."

Myrtle was not amused. "What's this fascinating assignment?"

Sloan's cheerfulness seemed forced. "The Bradley bake-off."

"Sloan, I do not wish to cover a cooking event."

Sloan quickly said, "But it gets pretty heated, Miss Myrtle. Those folks really slug it out."

"I'm assuming you're not speaking literally. The bake-off is quite a peaceful event."

"But you can feel the tension in the air," insisted Sloan.

Myrtle said sternly, "Red got to you, didn't he?"

Sloan swallowed loudly on the other end, as if his throat was parched. "Red?"

"My son, Red? The one who dislikes the fact that I'm a crime reporter?"

Sloan said, "The thing is, Miss Myrtle, your helpful hints column is a local favorite. Everyone is so excited when it comes out. I'd be delighted if you'd focus on that instead. Red mentioned that the investigation could get dangerous, and he didn't want you involved. Of course, I'd be totally devastated if anything happened to you. I have so many great memories of you in the classroom."

Now he really was fibbing. Myrtle decided he must be desperate.

"The fact of the matter is, I'm the natural candidate to cover this story. I was there. I've spoken with people. I knew Hortense. It would be silly for you to write it, as I presume you're suggesting."

Sloan said slowly, "I could write it and quote you in the article. Besides, Miss Myrtle, it's sort of a conflict of interest, isn't it? You're Red's mother. Won't it compromise the newspaper's integrity?"

Myrtle snorted. "Now you're really grasping at straws. You know I'm not going to write anything that lavishes praise on Red. Enough of this nonsense. I'm writing the story and that's that." She used her teacher voice.

"Got it," said Sloan miserably. "Okay. If you can get me the article in the next hour and a half, I'll run it in tomorrow's edition."

"Wonderful!" said Myrtle sweetly as she hung up the phone. Then she set to work writing the article.

Chapter Seven

That night she slept surprisingly soundly. She couldn't remember the last time she'd slept so well. Perhaps it had been time for her to catch up on all the many nights of lost sleep. Myrtle fixed herself a large breakfast and worked the crossword puzzle while she ate. She also admired her article, that was indeed right there on the front page of the paper. Several large cups of coffee later, she was ready to take on her day.

Around eight o'clock, she got a text message from Perkins. *I noticed your front porch light was out when I was driving away from Red's house last night. I think you usually keep it on?*

Myrtle wrote back that it must have burned out. That Red liked it on for security reasons and that she liked it on because of her middle-of-the-night strolls when insomnia hit.

Would you like me to run by the store and pick up a replacement bulb for you?

Myrtle smiled. Perkins was truly wonderful. His concern over her and his respectful attitude were always charming. Then she glowered at the fact that Perkins caught the burned-out bulb and Red hadn't. She was about to thank Perkins and ask him to buy the bulb, but then realized that Harold Daniels, Hortense's ex-husband, owned the hardware store. It sounded like the perfect excuse to be in the store. She told Perkins she appreciated the offer, but she would pick up the bulb herself.

Since it was such a reasonable hour, as opposed to the many times she'd called or dropped by Miles's house in the middle of the night, she set about calling Miles. "How's my sidekick this fine morning?"

Miles's voice was wary. "Fine. You sound . . . lively."

"Lively? Why yes, I suppose I am. That's because I had a luxurious night's sleep. It was simply lovely. But now I'm ready to get on to the task at hand."

"Which is?" asked Miles uneasily.

"Going to the hardware store."

Miles sounded relieved. "Oh, okay. You need something there?"

"I need a new lightbulb for my front porch. And I need to speak with Harold Daniels."

Miles sighed. "This is the Harold Daniels, who was married to Hortense, I suppose."

"Naturally, Miles. There couldn't be more than one Harold Daniels in a town the size of Bradley."

"And when are we interrogating this man?"

Myrtle said, "How about right now? Are you ready to go?"

Miles mumbled something under his breath, then said, "I'll be there in ten minutes."

Later, on the way to the hardware store, Myrtle regaled Miles with the story of her talk with Earl the previous day.

Miles said, "He's lost business because of Hortense's gossip?"

"That's what he said. He seemed rather discouraged about his prospects here, actually. He talked about moving from Bradley altogether and pursuing work near Charlotte."

Miles frowned. "That would be a pity. There aren't enough good yardmen in town as it is. In fact, I'd been mulling over finding another one, myself."

"Well, Earl does an excellent job, regardless of the whole weedkiller issue. That was an honest mistake. It's just a shame that he had to have such a lapse when he was in Hortense's yard."

Miles said slowly, "Hortense sounded intense."

"She was. Hortense was one of those women in garden club who I tried to avoid. I'm not saying she didn't know a lot about plants. But she was such a critical person. If you said you used a particular fertilizer, she'd tell you that another fertilizer was *much* better. If you showed her your prized tomato, she'd find some reason to find fault with it."

"She sounds like a real charmer," said Miles dryly.

"Well, I think she was one of those people who got along much better with plants than she did with people. Anyway, she apparently made Martha Green very upset by being critical of her flower arrangements. Martha thought it made Hortense unfit to be a grand judge at the flower show."

Miles said, "And so we suspect Martha might have murdered Hortense?"

"It does seem like a rather petty reason, doesn't it? But you have to understand that Martha puts a lot of stock into public recognition. She's the kind of person who isn't content with merely enjoying her flower arrangements herself. She wants to share them with others. Which is most unfortunate."

Miles raised an eyebrow. "I take it you're not fond of Martha's flower arrangements."

"They're horrid."

A smile curved Miles's lip. "That's your professional opinion?"

"I may not be a professional, but I know what's pretty and what isn't. And Martha's flowers are *not* pretty. Bless her heart."

Miles said, "What's wrong with them?"

"They're indescribable, Miles. You'll have to see them. I'm not going to attempt to put them into words." She looked sternly at Miles. "Going back to Earl, though. We were talking about Earl and we seemed to get very off-track. Earl was telling me that Harold acts as if his divorce from Hortense was fairly amicable. But Earl suspects he's the type of person who doesn't like being dumped. I guess Harold thinks a lot of himself."

Miles said, "Did he buy the hardware store from the previous owner?"

"No. The store has been in his family for ages."

"Harold seems like a pretty amiable guy. He's always very friendly when I go in there for air filters or whatnot," said Miles.

"Yes, he's certainly friendly. And very talkative. I remember having the dickens of a time trying to keep him from talking during English class. He was a total live wire."

Miles said, "I can't imagine trying to teach him English literature. That must have been tough going."

"As I recall, he didn't care much for Shakespeare."

"I can imagine," said Miles.

The hardware store was located right in downtown. It was a shop that had been in Harold's family for some time and sold everything from rather exotic-looking soft drinks in glass bottles, to live bait and everything in between. It transported Myrtle back in time as soon as she walked through the door of the two-story brick building. A brass bell chimed when Miles and Myrtle walked in. The wooden floors were made of worn and creaking wooden planks. It was a store where Myrtle took particular care to use her cane, since the floors were uneven.

Harold came right out to greet Myrtle. He was a man in his fifties, brash, and fond of loud golf shirts. "My favorite teacher! How are you today, Miss Myrtle?"

Myrtle beamed at him. "I'm doing excellently, Harold. This is my friend, Miles."

Harold stuck out his hand, and Miles reluctantly took it. Myrtle was sure he intended to use his hand sanitizer as soon as he could discreetly do so. "Good to meet you, Miles. Now, what can I do for the two of you today?"

Myrtle said sweetly, "Miles wanted to shop for a new garden hose nozzle."

Miles stared at her.

"Certainly! You've come to the right place. Now what sort of garden hose nozzle might you be looking for?"

Miles glared at Myrtle. "Myrtle will know."

"Goodness, Harold! You even stock different *types*. What kinds do you have?"

Harold puffed up in pride at his excellent selection. "Soaker hose nozzles, sweeper nozzles, dial hose nozzles, trigger nozzles, pistol grip nozzles, and rotating nozzles."

"Fascinating! Can you show them to us?"

Harold happily led the way, talking loudly about the store's gardening section. Miles leaned over and whispered, "I thought we were getting a lightbulb, Myrtle."

"That will give me an excuse to come back later. I may need to question Harold more than one time."

Miles, condemned to hear Harold's nozzle presentation, squared his shoulders. Harold gave his spiel, demonstrated the unique features of the nozzles, and then chirped, "So, what do you think, Miles? Did any catch your eye?"

Miles seemed remarkably unimpressed by any of the nozzles, but tried to summon some interest. "The, uh, cone nozzle was nice."

Harold beamed at him. "You're a discerning customer. A cone-shaped spray pattern is perfect for a variety of gardening tasks."

Miles endured the next couple of minutes of Harold lavishing praise on the cone nozzle. Then Harold finally, realizing the sale was wrapped up and there was no further need to wax poetic, smiled at Myrtle. "I forgot to ask how your family is doing, Miss Myrtle. Red and Elaine doing all right? And your grandson?"

"They're all doing splendidly. But I did want to extend my sympathies to you for Hortense's death."

Harold seemed quite a bit too jolly for someone who'd just suffered a loss, or at least some sort of jolt. He tried to be more somber, but the twinkle in his eyes remained. He snapped his fingers. "Gracious, Miss Myrtle. I just realized that you were the one who discovered Hortense yesterday. I hope it wasn't too hard for you to go through that. It must have been a terrible shock."

Myrtle thought it might sound too breezy to say she'd gotten accustomed to it. "It was, of course. An awful thing to happen."

Harold nodded gravely. "Yes. I spoke with Red about it yesterday. I was working late, and he came by to ask me a few questions." He gave them a smile. "I have the feeling I was a major suspect. I guess exes are usually pretty high on the suspect list. I was working at the hardware store, of course, when Hortense apparently died. Small business owners never have any time off, you know." He ruminated for a few seconds. "Actually, my long hours here were probably one of the death knells to my marriage to Hortense to begin with."

"I'm sure it was tough spending so much time apart," said Miles. He looked a lot more cheerful now that the interminable talk of nozzles was over with.

Harold nodded in agreement. "It sure was. Although it didn't help that I totally loathed yardwork and gardening. And Hortense couldn't have been less interested in hardware or my workshop where I built things. But I didn't want to lose Hortense, even though it felt like our relationship was coming to an end. I tried to get involved with the things she loved. I built trellises for her garden and even constructed a small greenhouse for her to grow some of her delicate seedlings. No matter how I tried, though, I could never get a positive reaction from her."

"It sounds as if it were an uphill battle," said Myrtle. "You ended up divorcing her."

Harold snorted. "*She* ended up divorcing *me*. But it was all very civil. We've also had a nice post-marriage relationship. In fact, Hortense provided me with one gift before she departed this world. She left everything to me."

"Gracious," said Myrtle. "That's very generous, considering the two of you were no longer in a relationship."

"Isn't it? I was doing all right financially before, but this means I'm looking at a completely different future. I might expand the store. I feel full of all kinds of possibilities. So, as you can see, I have no hard feelings toward Hortense at all. I understood she was seeing someone, and I was totally delighted for her, especially since the guy was a botanist. It sounded like he was the perfect match for her. And it's difficult to find a perfect match in a small town."

Myrtle said, "Since you knew Hortense so well, do you have any idea who might have done something like this to her? Did she have any enemies?"

Harold grinned at her. "Look at you with your reporter hat on. I guess I might read something about this in the paper, right?"

"The paper does *not* publish gossip. But it may help me have a better understanding of Hortense and perhaps offer some leads for the investigation."

"In that case," said Harold, "I'd say that the young girl who works over at the diner is probably the one with the biggest issue with Hortense. Emily White is her name. Cute girl, but she crossed Hortense. People shouldn't cross Hortense."

Miles said, "Hortense told you about the incident?"

"Oh, Hortense and I still talked, even after the divorce. But I mostly heard about it from garden club types coming into the hardware store. You know how gossip travels in Bradley."

The bell on the store's door rang, indicating another customer had come in. Miles was ready to leave. He said, "I should buy this nozzle and leave you to help other customers."

Harold completed the purchase, all the while cheerfully giving them a rundown on the sale items in the shop and the benefits of his frequent-buyer club. Soon, they were back outside the store on the sidewalk.

Miles said, "You know I don't have any need of a nozzle."

"It's a cheap enough purchase. You can gift it to Wanda, if you like. She's gotten very into gardening, you know, and I doubt she has very much equipment."

"Isn't Wanda wanting to find her own place here in Bradley? Apart from Crazy Dan?" asked Miles.

"She is, but there's been nothing on the market lately. Plus, anything that actually *is* on the market is overpriced. We'll wait until things settle down a little bit."

Miles said, "Got it. So, what now? Are we heading back to your place for some *Tomorrow's Promise*?"

"You're just as eager as I am to find out what happened, aren't you? I do have another errand to run, though, before we head back home. Would you take me to the store? I'd like to pick up some ingredients."

Miles looked uncomfortable. "Ingredients for what?"

"Aren't you nosy today! I'd like to make a lemon mousse for Arthur."

Miles's face seemed to ask who Arthur was and what he could possibly have done to Myrtle to make him deserve a lemon mousse.

"Arthur is Hortense's current amour. The botanist."

Miles asked, "Didn't you tell me they'd broken up? That Hortense had dumped him?"

"Yes, but that's even more reason to bake for him. He'll be upset for two different reasons, both having to do with Hortense."

Miles sounded uneasy. "Are you sure you should try attempting a lemon mousse? That sounds unnecessarily difficult. Why don't we pick up a dessert from the Piggly Wiggly? They have wonderful chocolate cakes."

Myrtle frowned. "I'd rather show him I put time, effort, and thought into the process. That may make Arthur open up more to me, out of gratitude."

Miles wasn't at all sure that was how it would work.

"Besides, it's not as if we have anything else on our agenda today. We might as well get a little baking done. Plus, it's cheaper to make food instead of buying it ready-made. I'm broke until my check comes, remember?"

Miles did not seem pleased by this. However, he dutifully drove Myrtle to the store and pushed the cart around as she pulled various ingredients off the shelf. "Shouldn't you be consulting a recipe?" he asked finally.

Myrtle waved her hand dismissively. "Not a bit. I've committed this recipe to memory. And my memory, as you know, is excellent."

"Excellent for most things. Fairly poor when it comes to ingredients."

Myrtle ignored him as she picked up marshmallows and threw them into the cart.

Miles said, "Was Wanda very disappointed when she found it was too pricy to move to Bradley?"

"Oh, you know Wanda. She has a good head on her shoulders. She was also saying that maybe it was a sign she needed to stay with her crazy brother and monitor him. But she's been socking away some money and thinks she may have enough for a used car. There was something about her being on retainer with a rich woman who calls her up for her fortune every day." Myrtle glanced over at Miles. "Actually, you'd be a lot of help with car shopping. You could tell us if a car was a clunker or not."

"I can try to help, but that's not really my area of expertise."

Myrtle said, "Being a CPA is close enough. At least you have financial experience."

"I was an engineer," said Miles in a chilly tone.

But Myrtle was not really listening. She was already heading for the checkout line. She somehow managed to produce two coupons from her purse related to her purchases, despite not having planned on making a dessert in advance. Miles frowned, as if suspecting that she might have altered the ingredients to suit the coupons she had.

"I can buy these things for you, you know," he said uncomfortably. "Or, if you think you might need more or different ingredients, I can take care of it for you."

"That's very generous of you, but I'm absolutely fine," said Myrtle in a cheerful voice.

Miles carried the bags to the car and put them into the back-seat. They headed off in the direction of Myrtle's house. "Regarding Wanda's car."

"Mm?"

"Isn't it sort of odd to talk about adding yet another car to Wanda's collection?" asked Miles. "Aren't there six or seven of them there, at least?"

"Yes, but none of them work. Many of them are sitting up on cinderblocks because they don't have tires. It would be better to get an *operational* car," said Myrtle as if explaining the problem to a very young child.

Miles said, "It seems maybe it would be a good idea to get the other cars towed to a junkyard. She might even get some extra cash that way."

Myrtle smiled at him. "It's very sweet how you're always concerned about Wanda. And I agree your plan makes sense. However, you're forgetting about the main problem."

"What's the main problem?"

"Her brother. Crazy Dan, as you know, is something of a hoarder. I have the feeling he would be very upset if his collection of inoperable cars suddenly disappeared from the yard. Plus, he seems determined to fill any sort of void by purchasing more things. You know what happened after Wanda cleared out the house?"

Miles sighed. "Yes. Dan went on an online buying spree."

"Precisely. But we'll keep our fingers crossed things will somehow improve. I'm sure living with Crazy Dan is very stressful for Wanda."

Several minutes later, they were back at Myrtle's house. Miles carried in the bags of groceries while Myrtle set up the television to show the recorded soap opera.

Chapter Eight

"You're not going to try to cook at the same time you're watching the show, are you?" Miles's voice was aghast.

"Why not? It's called multitasking. I can get a perfectly good view of the television from the kitchen counter. That way I can get this gelatin started, and we can find out what happens with the return of the evil twin."

Miles seemed uncomfortable. "Won't that be horribly distracting while you're trying to cook for Arthur?"

"Not at all. I handle multiple tasks excellently."

Miles said, "I've read articles that claim no one multitasks efficiently. Besides, there's no real hurry. You're not planning on seeing Arthur today, after all."

"But of course I am! There's no time like the present, Miles. I'd like to talk to all the major suspects in this investigation as soon as possible. Arthur, being Hortense's recently dumped boyfriend, has got to be at the top of the list now. You can come with me."

Miles muttered something under his breath that Myrtle couldn't quite catch.

"As my sidekick, you should show more enthusiasm. I bet we'll find out all sorts of interesting information from Arthur. Now, I'll put you in charge of the remote and fast-forwarding through the commercials. I'm going to get started in the kitchen."

"You'll pull the recipe out, won't you?" asked Miles, sounding anxious.

"It's imprinted on my memory."

Miles muttered under his breath again.

"Now let's get started with *Tomorrow's Promise*," said Myrtle in something of a bossy tone.

Miles started the show. He and Myrtle watched silently as Octavia embraced her twin, Vivienne. Vivienne said she'd start going by "Anastasia" now to distance herself from her dark past.

"She's going to need more than a name change to accomplish that," said Myrtle with a snort.

"How's the recipe coming?" asked Miles, as if trying to redirect her to the task at hand.

"Fine and dandy. Everything is boiling."

Miles frowned at this, but didn't press.

Soon, the soap opera showed all of Vivienne/Anastasia's evil plans through the use of her journal.

"Plot device!" sang out Myrtle from the kitchen.

"I'm not sure how else we'd know what's going through her head. She isn't being honest with any of the other characters about her intentions."

Vivienne/Anastasia's intentions were apparently to destroy her twin's entire existence. She was planning on rekindling a romance with Octavia's husband and then regain control of their family's vast fortune by convincing everyone that *Octavia* was actually the imposter.

Miles frowned. "Seems rather preposterous to me."

"Soap operas *are* preposterous. You have to suspend your disbelief."

"It gets harder and harder," said Miles. He paused. "How are things in the kitchen?"

"I believe I'm done. At least, I can't think of anything else that I need to do to the recipe."

Miles stood up and walked into the kitchen. "Aren't the marshmallows sort of gooey?"

"Just like s'mores."

Miles helpfully pointed out, "But you're not cooking s'mores. You're making gelatin. The marshmallows look rather odd."

"Why, they're just *fine*, Miles. Really."

Miles persisted. "May I see your recipe book?"

"Gracious, but you're obsessed with that recipe. For heaven's sake. All right." She walked to the cabinet, pulled it open, and thrust a tattered and food-stained old book at him.

Miles carefully flipped through it until he reached the recipe. "This mentions a cooling period. The syrup was supposed to cool before adding the gelatin."

"You're making this sound like a science experiment. It's baking."

Miles sighed. "Baking *is* a science experiment." He paused. "Did you put in an entire cup of sugar?"

"I just eyeballed it. I'm very good at estimates."

Miles looked doubtful at this.

"Let's finish up the show and take this right over to Arthur. I want to speak with him as soon as possible."

Miles hedged. "Maybe I should just drop you off at Arthur's house and then you could text me to pick you up. There are some errands I really need to run."

Myrtle frowned ferociously at him. "We were just out running an errand and you never said a word."

"It wasn't a grocery store errand."

Myrtle said, "I suspect you're simply very conveniently trying to get out of going with me to see Arthur. Which is too bad, because I won't allow you to renege on your responsibility as sidekick."

Miles unhappily watched the rest of the soap opera, all the while thinking about Arthur Wilkins getting a very disappointing lemon mousse.

Soon, they were back in the car, heading to Arthur Wilkins's house. "Which one is it?" asked Miles, peering down the street.

"You'll be able to tell right away. The clue is that he's a botanist."

Miles pointed. "That house."

"The very one."

Arthur Wilkins lived in a cottage that blended into the landscape. It was surrounded by dense woods, giving the impression that Arthur wanted the house to be part of the landscape. Vines climbed the walls of the cottage, creating a tapestry effect. Myrtle recognized clematis and ivy, then gave up even trying to identify the other vines. Potted plants lined the entrance.

"We'll have to ask for a tour," said Myrtle.

Miles frowned. "I thought we were trying to pass this off as a sympathy visit. Asking for a tour seems somewhat outside the parameters of that excuse."

"He'll love showing it off," assured Myrtle, carefully balancing the lemon mousse with one hand while gripping her cane with the other as she pulled herself out of the car. "Gracious, I nearly dropped the dessert."

"That would have been a pity," said Miles dryly.

They headed up Arthur's front walk, which was bordered by what was basically an English country garden, rife with flowers. Myrtle pressed the doorbell, and a minute later, Arthur opened the door. He had a very bookish air and wore thick glasses. His blond hair was completely disheveled. He actually looked as if he might have just woken from a nap.

"Miss Myrtle," he said with surprise, shoving a hand through his hair absently.

"Arthur, it's good to see you. Do you know my friend Miles?"

Arthur stuck out his hand, and Miles shook it. "Good to meet you, Miles. Won't the two of you come in?"

Myrtle swept inside. The inside of the house gave the impression that Arthur cared a great deal about plants and very little about possessions. "What a lovely place you have," said Myrtle. "But before I ask you all about your plants, let me give you this lemon mousse. We wanted you to know how very sorry we were about Hortense."

Miles quickly said, "Myrtle baked the mousse. I had nothing to do with it."

Arthur gave him a curious look. He said slowly, "Well, thank you so much, Miss Myrtle. That's awfully kind of you." He paused. "Hortense and I had just recently broken up, actually. You might not have heard the news about that."

"Oh, the gossip did reach me. But I figured the mousse could serve a double purpose. Sympathy for the breakup and sympathy for your loss." She proffered the dessert.

Miles watched as Arthur accepted it. Apparently, Miles's recusal of responsibility toward the dessert had made Arthur worried. His wariness indicated that he half-expected the mousse to explode at any minute.

"Thanks very much, Miss Myrtle. I'll look forward to enjoying that later."

Myrtle said, "Now, could you humor me and give us a tour of your cottage? You know I'm one of the garden club gals, and I would dearly love to see what you're growing here."

Arthur didn't seem taken aback by this request at all. He might have been used to showing people around, because he gave a practiced narrative as he talked about all the plants inside the house and out. Miles looked overwhelmed by the sheer number of green things growing in pots on every available surface, but Myrtle steered herself through the jungle with ease, asking intelligent questions about everything Arthur had there.

When Arthur had finished his tour, he seemed to be about to thank them, in a pointed manner, for coming over. But Myrtle sat herself down in an old armchair before he could get the words out. She said, "My, my. Such a terrible thing, wasn't it?"

Arthur looked baffled by the non sequitur. "A terrible thing?"

"Poor Hortense's death. Shocking. You know I discovered her. Well, along with my psychic friend."

The sudden mention of psychics seemed to make Arthur even more confused than he already was. "Sorry, you were the one who found Hortense's body yesterday?"

"That's right. I'd slipped away from the opening remarks in order to get an early preview of the plants at the show." She paused before saying sweetly, "I'm positive you were there at the show, too. As expected. You're so interested in plants of all kinds that I knew you'd want to make an appearance at the flower show. I do hope my Red hasn't been giving you a hard time, since you didn't have an alibi for the event."

Arthur now looked somewhat irritated. "I wasn't at the flower show whatsoever. I'd thought about sticking my head in briefly to view the orchids, but then I got wrapped up with a project I'm currently working on."

"You weren't there? I'm surprised you didn't arrive at the recreation center bright and early with bells on."

Arthur seemed blindsided at being unexpectedly interrogated. "I'd been working on a request by a state conservation organization. They wanted me to identify an unusual plant that had been located in a remote area of North Carolina. I'd gotten caught up in my research and hadn't checked the time."

Myrtle raised her eyebrows. "You must really have been fascinated with whatever you were researching."

"I was. I often get such queries from officials, but this one was particularly interesting. When I realized what time it was, I decided I wouldn't go to the flower show at all. It was only going to get busier over there the later it was. I'm not fond of those types of shows, anyway. Of course, the downside was that I'd purchased a ticket, and it would go to waste. Also, Hortense would have thought I'd avoided the show because I was at home sulking over our breakup. I decided avoiding the crowds was still worth the downsides of not attending."

The expression on Arthur's face indicated that what Hortense made of his absence was a most undesired outcome.

Myrtle again asked sweetly, "Why would Hortense have thought you were sulking? I thought you were the one who ended things with her."

The botanist said shortly, "That wasn't the case."

"Was the relationship ended by joint agreement?" pushed Myrtle, looking interested.

Arthur appeared even more aggravated then. He said, "No, I was dumped by Hortense, if that's what you want to know."

Miles cleared his throat. He was either trying to stop their visit from being prematurely terminated or trying to change the subject. "I'd be interested in hearing more about your work as a botanist."

Myrtle said, "I'm surprised you have such an interest in the subject, Miles. I'd have thought architects wouldn't have been interested in the vagaries of plants."

"Engineer," muttered Miles darkly.

Arthur rattled off an overview of his thrilling life as a botanist, which included flying out to conferences for lectures, writing a few important papers, and penning one well-received book.

When he finished his monologue, Myrtle said, "My, that's a lot of work. Do you also regularly attend events like the flower show? I know you mentioned they weren't your favorites."

"I don't usually take a lot of pleasure in them, no. I appreciate more of a scientific analysis of flowers. Flower shows are all about design, art, and aesthetics. Actually, I enjoy attending agricultural conferences more."

Myrtle said, "Going back to your breakup. Do you feel any bitterness toward Hortense and the way the relationship soured?"

"Not a bit," said Arthur stiffly. "I felt as if we were soulmates. We seemed to share a lot in an academic sense and had a good deal of respect for each other. I'd envisioned a future with Hortense and was startled when she tired of me and decided to end the relationship. I was sorry it ended, but I wasn't bitter. If Hortense felt the relationship was over, there was no reason for me to try to prolong it."

Myrtle said, "I'm assuming Red spoke with you. Were you able to give him a suggestion for an alternate suspect?"

"An alternate suspect?" Arthur began looking longingly at the door, as if wishing he could hustle his guests in that direction.

"That's right. Basically, I'm asking if you know of anyone who might have had a grudge against Hortense. Maybe someone who simply didn't like her very much. We're just trying to piece together what might have happened to her."

Arthur said, "Yeah, there's one person who comes to mind. Hortense had inherited her mother's house and hadn't wanted to sell the thing. A local investor pleaded with her to sell it, but she'd hang up the phone on the guy."

"Do you remember who the investor was?" asked Miles.

Arthur pursed his lips, trying to remember. Then he said, "Nope. Nothing's coming to mind, I'm afraid. Anyway, after he tried sweet-talking Hortense, he started really haranguing her. It made her pretty cranky. More than that, though, it put Hortense's back up. She got really stubborn when people tried to tell her what to do. He only made her more resolved *not* to sell it."

"I wonder what happens to the property now?" mused Myrtle.

"From what I hear, Hortense's entire estate is going to Harold, her ex-husband." Arthur shook his head. "Guess she never got around to updating her will after her marriage fell apart."

"I hear their parting was quite amicable," said Myrtle.

Arthur snorted. "Where did you hear that from? Oh, never mind—you must have spoken with Harold. Hortense never would have said they had a friendly divorce. She was determined to move on as quickly as possible, which is why she ended up in a relationship with me so fast."

"Hortense spoke poorly of Harold?" asked Miles.

"She couldn't stand the guy. She said they argued over many things and had nothing at all in common. Hortense would cross the street to avoid Harold, and that's the truth."

Miles cleared his throat. "Going back to the investor. Was he wanting to use the property for residential housing?"

"Hortense said he wanted to build an office building there. It's at the edge of downtown and is zoned for residential or business. It sure seems like an excellent motive for murder to me."

It did to Myrtle, too. She stood up, and Arthur looked at her in relief. "I'm afraid it's time for Miles and me to head out. But it was lovely catching up with you, despite the terrible circumstances."

"Thank you, Miss Myrtle," said Arthur soberly. He walked her toward the door to ensure she didn't change her mind about leaving.

Chapter Nine

Soon, Myrtle and Miles were back in Miles's car again. "That was fairly informative," said Myrtle.

"Was it?" asked Miles as he backed up down the driveway. "I thought Arthur was obfuscating."

"Naturally. All the suspects do, of course. It's interesting that Hortense and Harold didn't have the peaceful divorce that Harold claimed they did. And this investor seems like an interesting lead." She paused. "I wonder if I could do some sort of information trade with Perkins. Perhaps I could offer him what I know about the investor and get some forensics details in return."

"Well, I know for a fact that wouldn't work with Red. I doubt the tactic will work with Perkins, either."

Myrtle took out her phone to find out. She animatedly filled in Perkins. Then she listened, crestfallen. "I see. No, that's no problem at all. The porch light? No, I haven't gotten around to buying the bulb yet. Okay."

Miles pulled the car into Myrtle's driveway. "From your expression, it looks as if the information exchange didn't go quite as well as you'd hoped."

"Not a bit. It's all very aggravating. They'd already spoken with this investor, and he has an ironclad alibi. Apparently, he was in Vienna."

Miles said dryly, "That does appear to be a fairly substantial alibi."

"There are ways around an alibi, however, especially for someone with means. He could easily have contracted someone to kill Hortense. It could have been a professional hit."

"However, a flowerpot would be an unusual weapon for an assassin to use. I'd imagine they would be fonder of .22 handguns. Perhaps with a silencer," said Miles.

"Don't be such a smarty-pants. It's just extremely annoying for a lead to go caput like this."

Miles asked, "Perkins didn't give you any information in return, I take it?"

"No, he politely said he needed to keep the forensics findings under his hat. Most discouraging."

They walked into Myrtle's house just as her cell phone started ringing. She brightened. "Perhaps Perkins has had second thoughts."

But it was Red. Myrtle glanced over at Miles and rolled her eyes as Red said, "Mama, stay out of my case. I know you just called Perkins."

Myrtle frowned. "I didn't have Perkins down as a tattletale."

"He's not. But I overheard part of his phone conversation. He doesn't have time to deal with you on top of this case."

Myrtle gritted her teeth. "He's not *dealing* with me. We're just having little talks from time to time."

"Well, these little talks need to stop." Red's voice became gentler. "Actually, I know a way you can really help out. In fact, I need your help."

This was unusual. So unusual that Myrtle was suspicious. "Pray tell."

"Elaine's neck is doing better, but it's still pretty messed up. The muscle relaxer helps, but it makes her super-sleepy. She doesn't want to ask for help."

"But that's silly!" said Myrtle. "I told her to reach out to me right away if she needed help of any kind."

"She told me she doesn't want to bother you. Anyway, she could use some help."

Myrtle's brain was already planning all the different ways she could be of assistance. "I could run her errands for her. Cooking a meal is a no-brainer, of course."

Red's voice was just as alarmed as Miles's face now was. "Mama, there's no need for cooking. Or errands. All I'm suggesting is that you take Jack off her hands for a while. That'll do you both some good. No cooking, got it?"

"Mm-hmm." But Myrtle wasn't really listening. Red made a hasty goodbye, saying he had to get off the phone.

Myrtle said, "You know, I think doing a little more cooking would do me some good. It's great for stress relief. I love the creative process."

Miles was shaking his head. "I'm not sure cooking is supposed to be as creative as you're making it out to be. I think it's more about following a recipe."

"Nonsense. The recipe is a mere suggestion."

Miles said, "You heard Red. He said he didn't want you cooking. Anyway, you'll be better off helping Elaine with Jack. I can't imagine having to care for someone else when you're feeling that uncomfortable."

"There's no reason I can't do two things at once."

Miles now said desperately, "There's one good reason. If you cook for them, you'll have to go back to the store. You've told me you're tight on cash until your check comes in."

"Which is, sadly, very true. However, that doesn't mean that I can't come up with a lovely, nutritious meal from the items I have here in the house." She waltzed into the kitchen and opened her cabinets. Miles could see a hodge-podge of food, including corn flakes, olives, canned chicken, and asparagus. He shivered, feeling a visceral reaction at all the horrid possibilities.

Which was when Myrtle's phone rang again.

"Mercy! I'm so very popular this Sunday." She glanced at the phone and started smiling. "Wanda!"

"Hi Myrtle."

"How are things going over there?"

Wanda said, "They're all good. That woman paid me lots to tell her fortune."

"The wealthy woman who thinks you're her own personal seer? I'm glad she's proving to be an excellent source of income. Is the Sight working better with a bit of money thrown at it?"

Wanda gave a wheezing chuckle. "Reckon it is. At any rate, good enough." She paused. "Matter of fact, the Sight gave me a message jest seconds ago. Thought I'd better call you up."

"Did it, indeed? How wonderful! What did it say?"

Wanda said, "It's sorta weird. Jest a vision of Red, Elaine, and Jack eatin' takeout."

Miles, who could hear both ends of the conversation, just smiled.

"That *is* very odd. Takeout? But I was planning on cooking for them all. I've got a motley assortment of foodstuffs here and was going to throw it all together.

Miles shuddered.

"Jest lettin' you know they'll end up with takeout. Wouldn't want to mess with the way things is supposed to be."

Myrtle said slowly, "No, that's very true. I don't need to function as some sort of cosmic disruptor." She paused. "Perhaps Red needs the opportunity to be the hero by bringing food back home. He did sound very concerned about Elaine, but can't be a help to her with a murder investigation going on. That's very helpful, Wanda, thank you. Was there anything else you saw from the Sight?"

"Yer in danger."

"Naturally. Well, thanks for this, Wanda."

"Take care, Myrtle."

Miles was now looking vastly relieved. "If you're going to help with Jack, I should get out of your hair."

"Yes, that might be for the best. I'll probably head across the street and forcibly take Jack from her hands. I know she doesn't want to be any trouble, but it's so silly for her to be reticent to accept help."

Miles walked home as Myrtle set out across the street to collect her grandson. Several hours later, they were still playing

Memory, watching cartoons, and singing loads of children's songs.

As much as Myrtle loved her time with Jack, she was astonished at how tiring it was to play full time with someone who wasn't yet four. After Red collected him, it was all Myrtle could do to stay awake until it was closer to bedtime. She nearly fell asleep playing solitaire, nodded off over her crossword puzzle book, and even watching the evil twin episode a second time didn't keep her from snoozing. Finally, she dropped into bed around eight-thirty, figuring it was as close as she could manage to her normal bedtime. This naturally meant she was wide-awake at three o'clock in the morning.

Myrtle knew better than to fight the insomnia. She got right up, putting on her robe and slippers. The problem was that she had done all of her usual time-passers the night before and was in no mood to continue watching TV, doing crosswords, or playing cards. It was sadly too early for the morning paper to have arrived, which would have been another diversion. Thus stymied, she headed out the door and set off for Miles's house.

She smiled when she saw a light on. Miles was having trouble sleeping, too. She rang the doorbell, and he appeared at the door wearing a navy bathrobe over striped pajamas. "I rather thought you might come over," he said. "I put a pot of coffee on and set out some croissants."

They settled in Miles's tidy kitchen. Miles brought butter and jam to the table and poured the coffee.

"How did things go with Jack?"

Myrtle beamed at him. "We had the best time ever. I know you wished you lived closer to your grandkids. They really are so much fun."

Miles looked a bit wistful. "Having them closer than California would be nice. Although I did have a video call with Ben and Ethan. That was nice."

"No Dana?" asked Myrtle, referring to Miles's daughter.

"She was working, unfortunately."

"I suppose as a physician and an attorney, there's a lot of work happening," said Myrtle. She found Dana very nice when she'd met her. Although she did think she was quite an overachiever. "I suppose having teenaged grandchildren isn't quite as tiring. At least, you're likely not making forts."

"I wouldn't think so, no," said Miles. "Although we did play a multiplayer video game online."

"How very enterprising of you, Miles! One of those shooting games?"

Miles said, "I think they realized my reflexes likely weren't up to the challenge. It was a multiplayer online game of hearts."

"Ah," said Myrtle. "Well, at least you were able to hang out with them. I did so enjoy my time with Jack. The only thing is that I became inexplicably exhausted. I turned in ridiculously early, which is why I woke up so early."

Miles nodded. "I don't even have an excuse for being up at three. My insomnia has been worse lately."

"Perhaps we should have a really full day today and then force ourselves to stay up until eleven p.m. That might stop the vicious cycle."

Miles said, "But you had an over-full day yesterday, and it didn't seem to work at all. I do have one thing I needed to do today. I'm to run over to speak with Earl Jenkins."

Myrtle raised her eyebrows, looking archly at Miles. "You're thinking of contracting a potential killer to be your new yardman?"

"I don't think Earl seems all that dangerous. And I'm not sure that being fired by someone is a great motive for killing them."

Myrtle said, "The bigger problem is that Hortense was telling everyone in town what happened. She was trying to ruin Earl's professional reputation. He was most distressed over it."

"Well, I'm sure it wouldn't be a great business model if Earl started killing off his customers. I believe I'll be completely safe if I hire him. The only problem is that he doesn't have a cell phone. I'll have to run by his house."

Myrtle blinked at this. "Doesn't have a *phone*? How does one even run a business without a phone?"

"He said he just doesn't like phones. He knocks on his customers' doors if he needs to speak to them."

Myrtle said, "What an extraordinary way to work. And extraordinary that you want him doing work for you."

"Like I mentioned earlier, I've been thinking about having a new service for some time. The guy I'm using has just raised his rates and doesn't seem to do a careful job."

Myrtle said, "Dusty's worked for you before."

"And it worked out better than I thought. But I'd rather have someone more predictable."

"I could come along with you, Miles. That way, I could question Earl again. I'm not at all sure he was as sanguine as he pretended to be about Hortense firing him. I could picture him snapping at the flower show and taking out Hortense with a pot."

Miles shook his head. "If I'm going to convince the man to take me on as a new customer, I don't need him being interrogated by my friend. I'll fill you in on any salient details I discover . . . if there *are* any, which I doubt."

So Myrtle was left to her own devices. Fortunately, Pasha dropped by for a snuggle and a can of tuna. That was distracting for a while. But life was becoming quite dull again when Myrtle's phone rang.

"Miles?" she asked. "That didn't take long. Will Earl take over as your new yardman?"

"He won't be doing anyone's yard anymore," said Miles grimly. "He's dead."

Myrtle felt Miles didn't have quite the amount of experience that she did in discovering bodies. "Are you certain? Earl isn't just sleeping? Gardening is tough work."

"Unfortunately, it was pretty clear that he is very, very dead."

Myrtle said, "Mercy. What on earth is going on? I'm coming right over, of course."

"There's really no need for that. I'm sure Red won't want to see you at another crime scene."

"Nonsense. I don't desert my friends in their hours of need." She hung up and hurried across the street to ask Elaine if she could borrow her minivan. She offered to run Elaine's errands after she met up with Miles. But Elaine didn't seem to have any errands to run.

"Has something happened?" asked Elaine. "Red was here at the house to grab a bite to eat, but then he suddenly raced away."

"Miles found a body," said Myrtle. "Which is fairly unusual. Miles hasn't found as many bodies as I have." Myrtle was born with a healthy sense of competion.

"Oh no. Who is it this time?"

"Earl Jenkins, the landscaper."

Elaine gave Myrtle her keys. Myrtle snuggled Jack for a few seconds, then headed for the car. She sat in the driver's set for another couple of moments, reacquainting herself with all the buttons. Finally, deciding she was fine as long as it didn't start raining, she set off for Earl Jenkins's house. Or where she hoped she remembered correctly where his house was. His family had been there for ages, but she wasn't sure she could recall the precise location.

In the end, it didn't matter if she remembered the precise location or not. Earl's small home had been invaded by all sorts of emergency personnel. There were blue lights and red lights flashing from all the vehicles. Myrtle pulled up as close as she could in the minivan, then hopped out to find Miles. She soon located him, propped up on his car and looking unhappy.

"How did you get here so fast?" asked Miles. "This isn't even very close to home."

"I borrowed Elaine's minivan again. Now, tell me exactly what happened."

Miles shook his head. "There's really not that much to tell. I showed up and knocked on Earl's door. When he didn't answer, I figured he was probably working in his own yard."

"I'm guessing his car was here."

"That's right," said Miles. "When I saw the car, I knew he was probably at home. So I walked around the side of the house, and there he was." Miles grimaced.

"Dead. But murdered? Or dead from some sort of coronary event?"

Miles looked even more unhappy. "Decidedly murdered. With some sort of vintage scythe."

"Mercy. How very dramatic."

Miles said, "I suppose it was one of Earl's own tools. He apparently had a collection of them in his storage shed."

Myrtle, who'd been looking around as they spoke, suddenly raised her eyebrows. "Well, look who's coming our way."

"Not Red," said Miles with a groan. "I've already spoken with him once today."

"Arthur Wilkins. Our friendly neighborhood botanist and Hortense's ex-boyfriend. How very interesting that he's here."

Chapter Ten

Arthur looked harried, disconcerted, and very much in his own head. He was so focused on his own thoughts that Myrtle had to call his name several times before he turned his head and headed in their direction.

"Miss Myrtle? Miles? What are the two of you doing here?" He didn't actually look altogether happy to see them.

Myrtle said sweetly, "I might ask you the same thing."

"I was driving by and saw all the emergency vehicles. Earl had been helping me maintain my yard when I've had to go out of town for lectures and things. I wanted to find out what happened." His frown deepened. "And now I've learned that Earl is dead."

"Upsetting, isn't it?" asked Myrtle, although she seemed entirely unfazed by Earl's sudden demise. "Miles here found him."

Arthur now turned his angry gaze Miles's way, as if it were all his fault. "What were you doing over here?"

Miles said, "Just trying to engage his services for my own yard. I understood he didn't do business by phone."

"Very true. He was an unusual man. And now I've got to find a new yardman." He looked at Myrtle. "Does Red do your yard?"

"Red? Heavens, no. I wouldn't want him at my house that often. No, Dusty is my man."

Arthur nodded. "I think I've seen him around. Does he do a good job?"

Myrtle snorted. "It depends on what you call a good job. He's very good at using the weed whacker around my gnome collection, and he's not expensive. The problem is that he's lazy. It's very difficult to get him to come out to one's house. I couldn't, in good conscience, recommend him."

"I'd better look elsewhere, then. That would only aggravate me."

Myrtle said, "It's a shame about Earl. I suppose the police will be speaking with you about it soon."

Arthur scowled at her. "Why would they? I certainly didn't want to kill Earl. His death is creating nothing but trouble and inconvenience for me."

"As a rule, the police speak to suspects again when another death occurs. But maybe you have an alibi for this morning."

Arthur shook his head. "I was doing necessary drudgery at home. Catching up on housework, caring for my plants. Then I started to prepare for a presentation I'm giving that will help determine environmental policy and regulations."

Myrtle said, "What does that entail?"

"Oh, coming up with talking points relating to plant conservation and natural resource management." Arthur seemed rather smug at having such an important task.

"I see. Good luck with your work on that."

Arthur added, "Thanks. In terms of an alibi, if I'd known Earl was going to be murdered, I'd have made sure I was in a specific location where everyone could see me. But I wasn't, because I had no idea Earl was going to suddenly perish. I can't do anything about how it looks. The police will simply believe whatever they believe. They won't have any evidence, because I didn't kill anyone."

Myrtle nodded sadly. "Naturally. Poor Earl. And now the local chatterboxes are moving on to talking about you and how you might have murdered Hortense. It would be nice to put all the local gossip to bed, wouldn't it?"

Arthur knit his brows. "People are gossiping? About *me*?" He seemed outraged by the idea.

"You know how Bradley is."

"It's a gossipy place. But if they actually asked me to my face, I would tell them I bore no ill-will toward Hortense. She was free to do whatever she wanted, as was I."

Myrtle said, "Of course. It's just that the story that's circulating is that you were a lot more upset about the breakup than you're making out."

"That sounds like libel to me." Arthur's voice was peeved. "I'm not sure 'upset' is the right word, anyway. Our breakup stung. Of course it stung. I thought Hortense and I made a good couple. We had plenty of things in common and shared a similar intellect. We enjoyed many of the same things."

Myrtle thought Arthur made it sound as if he were checking things off a checklist, or taking into consideration the purchase of an expensive plant.

"Besides, I was nowhere near the show when Hortense was killed. As I mentioned to you, I set off late for the event."

Myrtle managed to look sorrowful. "Except that someone, and I can't for the life of me remember who, says that they saw you there that morning." This was a fib, but Myrtle wanted to see how he reacted to it. Perhaps Arthur would hang his head and admit to being at the flower show.

Myrtle's hopes were dashed as Arthur said, "But that's not true! Libel, again! They must have mistaken me for someone else."

Myrtle gave him a doubtful look.

"See?" said Arthur. "Even you don't believe me. Nobody would." He hunched his shoulders up and looked annoyed. "People are the worst. This is exactly why I'm spending so much time with my plants. Or at conferences where scientists are in attendance and actually understand what I do and enjoy learning about it. There's just too much drama in everyday life."

Arthur narrowed his eyes and said forcefully, "Miss Myrtle, I don't know where you got your information, but I can assure you that I was not at that flower show."

"Because your research was so very interesting?" Myrtle allowed her voice to reflect some uncertainty.

"Yes, actually, although I know research may not sound like a fun activity to amateurs. You see, the North Carolina Department of Agriculture requested my help. This is the first time they've asked me to step in to identify the potential ecological impacts of a plant species."

Miles was looking as if he might be in urgent need of coffee.

Arthur forged ahead with great determination. "I've been gathering data regarding the plant's growth patterns, habitat, and behavior. It's proven to be a tricky subject, but I'm making strides in understanding it." He scowled in annoyance. "And now it seems the universe is intent on distracting me. My landscaper has been murdered. And I somehow appear to be a suspect in a homicide investigation."

"Maybe you wouldn't be as much of a suspect if you could give a solid idea as to who might have wanted to kill Hortense and Earl."

Arthur said, "Well, the last time we spoke, I told you it was probably that investor who wanted to buy that house from Hortense."

Myrtle said coolly, "It appears that investor has an excellent alibi since he was in Austria at the time. Is there anyone else you can think of?"

Arthur threw up his hands. "Sure. What about Hortense's ex-husband? Those two fought like cats and dogs. I don't think Harold ever got over Hortense, no matter what he says."

Myrtle said, "Really? Harold makes out that he and Hortense got along well."

"They didn't. I overheard plenty of arguments, both on the phone and in-person. Harold was always squabbling over one thing or another and seemed insanely jealous about Hortense's relationship with me. And now, Harold has been blabbing all over town that Hortense left her money and property to him." Arthur gave a short laugh.

Miles said, "Did Hortense intend to do that?"

"No way." barked Arthur. "She just didn't take the time to update her will. Hortense hated doing administrative stuff. She'd rather be messing around with her plants. She'd put off doing things she didn't want to do. Plus, she probably thought she'd live decades longer."

Arthur looked over at the large gathering in Earl's yard and shifted uncomfortably. "They're looking over here at us."

Myrtle peered over at Earl's yard. "Oh, that's just Red. Glowering at me."

"We should probably leave," said Miles.

"Has Red already spoken with you, Miles?" asked Myrtle.

"Red *and* Perkins. They told me I was free to leave. I think that was a hint that they'd like me to head out. The only reason I stayed is because you were on your way over."

Arthur was already heading for his vehicle. "See you later," he said hastily, clearly not wanting another conversation with the police.

Myrtle said to Miles, "Want to head to my house? I'll make more coffee."

Miles nodded. "Sure. I'll follow you there. I'm guessing you need to drop the minivan by Elaine's house."

"I could follow you," said Myrtle.

"I'd rather you set the pace."

Myrtle frowned. "Are you disparaging the speed in which I drive?"

"I wouldn't dream of it."

Myrtle climbed into the minivan and carefully started the car. She put on her blinker to indicate she was heading into the street. As she cautiously checked her rearview mirrors, she saw

Red's face. He looked apoplectic at the sight of his mother in his wife's minivan again. "Needs to take his blood pressure medicine," she muttered to herself.

Before long, she'd delivered Elaine's minivan safely back in her driveway and walked across the street to her home. There was a large box in front of her door, and she smiled to herself.

Miles pushed his glasses up his nose as he surveyed the box. "A bench for your backyard?"

"Not even. Keep guessing."

"A potted plant for your living room? A set of new pillows?"

Myrtle shook her head, smiling.

"Not new equipment for your kitchen." Miles was looking leery now.

"You'll never guess. We'll just have to open it."

Miles said, "Shall I carry it inside, then?"

"No, it'll be better to keep it on the front porch. I'll grab my box cutter and let you do the honor."

Myrtle returned with a bright red box cutter, and Miles carefully cut the tape. He opened the box to reveal a large Elvis gnome.

"Isn't he wonderful? Look at his precious face," said Myrtle.

The gnome sported a slick pompadour and a miniature white bedazzled jumpsuit. He had distinctive sideburns, arched eyebrows, and a playful smile curled on its lips. To cap it off, it wore a pair of blue suede-looking shoes.

Miles studied the gnome. "Well, you can definitely tell it's Elvis. This must have been rather an expensive purchase."

"That's the very best part! It didn't cost me a cent. I received an online gift card from a former student who made it big in

New York. He said he wanted to give something to his favorite teacher as a thank you. And he did." Myrtle gave a smug smile.

"What does he do in New York?"

Myrtle said vaguely, "Something to do with stocks. On Wall Street."

"Surely he'd have wanted to thank his math or business teacher, then."

Myrtle glared at him. "No, he'd want to thank the teacher who encouraged him to get his work done and stop messing around. I told him he was far too smart to engage in the type of behavior he was demonstrating."

"Got it. Want me to lug Elvis into the storage shed with the other gnomes?"

Myrtle said, "Absolutely not. He's going right into my front yard, front and center. I want to make sure Red has an excellent view of him."

Miles lifted an eyebrow. "A solo performance? Usually, you call Dusty to get the entire gnome army out."

"If anyone deserves a solo, it's Elvis."

Miles set Elvis out in the yard. Myrtle asked him to move the gnome several times until she was satisfied with his location.

They walked inside. "What was Red's infraction this time?" asked Miles.

"Hmm?"

"What did Red do to deserve being gnomed?" clarified Miles.

"Oh, the usual stuff. Bossing me around. Being so horrified when I was driving Elaine and Jack to the drugstore. That type of thing. He's so very annoying."

A car stopped outside. Miles pushed the sheer curtains aside. He remarked, "Someone is taking a selfie with your Elvis."

Myrtle brightened. "That's nice. What Red doesn't understand is that my gnomes provide a little ray of sunshine in people's lives."

"I suppose he's only thinking that it makes his blood pressure go up."

Myrtle shook her head. "He really needs to monitor his blood pressure better. I could tell it was sky high when I left the crime scene in his minivan."

"It was likely the juxtaposition of 'crime scene,' 'you,' and 'minivan' that was the problem."

Myrtle said, "I suppose. He should just get over it. Now, let's take care of you for a moment."

Miles looked surprised at this. "Me?"

"Of course! I do know how to be a good friend, you realize. You've had a most unsettling morning. In fact, it's nearly lunchtime now. How about if I make you a tomato sandwich? And we'll have a nice bowl of ice cream for dessert. Then we can watch today's episode of *Tomorrow's Promise* live."

Now Miles seemed suspicious. "What's the catch?"

"The *catch*? Can't I just be nice to my friend?"

Miles tilted his head, looking doubtful. "You're wanting me to go somewhere with you this afternoon, aren't you?"

"Only when you're fully recovered from your distress." Myrtle busied herself in the kitchen for a few minutes while Miles readied the television for the soap opera. Soon Myrtle had made the sandwiches and scooped a large scoop of ice cream into two small glass bowls. Miles helped her carry the food and their ice waters into the living room.

Tomorrow's Promise was, if anything, even more outlandish than it had been the day before. Mysterious crop circles appeared overnight in the town's fields, and reports of cattle abductions flooded the local police department. Then the evil twin might somehow be in cahoots with the aliens.

Miles shook his head. "That episode was like a fever dream."

"Perhaps the writers are on drugs," said Myrtle with a frown. "Maybe they'll redeem themselves tomorrow with a better storyline. Shall we head off on our little mission?"

"You never revealed what our little mission was."

"Didn't I?" asked Myrtle. "We're going to pay a visit to Martha Green."

Miles made a face. "Must we?"

Myrtle's eyes twinkled. "You don't have to have that reaction, you know. Martha is a perfectly lovely person, even if she spends a good deal of time flirting with you."

Miles flushed. "She just enjoys seeing me look uncomfortable. Besides, what excuse do we have to drop in on Martha? And why, again, do you think Martha is a suspect?"

"I thought I'd explained all that to you. Martha was upset that Hortense disparaged her arrangements at every opportunity. She also believed that Hortense wasn't a good choice for being the head judge of the flower show. I know we said it was a petty reason, but then Martha can be a rather petty person."

Miles asked, "And our pretense for the visit?"

"At garden club, Martha said her daylilies needed to be divided. She offered them to anyone who wanted to come over and get them."

"So now we have to dig," said Miles glumly.

"I'm not the one in nice clothes. You could change, you know."

Miles looked down at his carefully pressed khakis and his button-down shirt. He didn't appear enthusiastic about changing clothes. "I suppose I could."

"Go put on your play clothes and then come back over."

Fifteen minutes later, Miles returned, looking much the same as he had before. Myrtle frowned. "Did you even change?"

"Yes. These are a pair of my oldest khakis. I paired them with an old button-down."

Myrtle peered at the garments. "Aside from a tiny bit of fraying, they look perfect. They'd qualify as top-tier clothes in my closet. But let's set off. I want to be sure to catch Martha before she runs any Monday errands."

"Shouldn't we be bringing gardening gloves and spades?"

"Mercy, you're right, Miles. Could you grab them out of the shed for me?"

Miles disappeared for a couple of minutes, then returned with the garden tools. They set off, passing someone taking a picture of the Elvis gnome from their parked car.

"I think you're going to be a celebrity," said Miles dryly.

"I'm *already* a celebrity."

"From your stories in the paper?" asked Miles.

"Because I taught nearly everyone in town over age thirty-five," said Myrtle. Although she very much liked the idea of being a celebrity journalist. "But you've reminded me I need to work on my next story for the *Bugle* as soon as I get back home."

Chapter Eleven

Martha's house was a white two-story home with columns at the front. It was, in every way, very similar to Tippy's house, if a bit smaller. Her yard was kept very tidy and sported separated beds of perennials and annuals. There was an English country garden in the back that was lovely; however, Martha apparently thought it wasn't tidy-looking enough to go in the front of the house.

They walked up to the generous verandah, and Myrtle rang the doorbell. Martha opened the door with a huge grin on her face. She seemed to shimmer as she looked at Miles, who increasingly looked as if he wanted to head back to the safety of his vehicle.

"How wonderful! My friends are here. What a very happy Monday surprise! Come in, come in."

Myrtle swept inside, heading for Martha's light-filled sunroom. "I hope you don't mind us dropping by, Martha."

"No, of *course* not. This will be the highlight of my day." Martha busied herself by tidying an already-neat stack of gardening magazines on a small glass table.

Myrtle said, "We're planning on dividing up some of your daylilies for you. Unless they've all been divided and taken by other garden club members."

"I have lots and lots for you to divide. You can take your pick. Each one has a little sign in front, telling you what type of daylily it is."

It all sounded very much like Martha. She waved at the chairs, indicating they should take a seat. "Now, what can I get you to drink? I have fresh-squeezed lemonade, fresh-squeezed orange juice, iced tea, regular tea, coffee, water, or bloody Marys."

Myrtle said, "I think just water, dear."

Miles gave Martha a small smile. "I'm actually not thirsty."

Martha looked devastated that Miles didn't take her up on her offer. Myrtle said, "Miles, you were just telling me recently that you wanted to hydrate more. Here's your chance."

"Water, then, please," said Miles obediently.

Martha hurried off. Soon she was back with a large tray of drinks, blueberry muffins, and various cheeses and crackers. "I thought we might want a snack while we visited."

Miles was looking unhappily at his "old" khakis and button-down, as if he wished he'd dressed up more for the occasion. Myrtle knew Martha was thinking she could snare Miles by showing him what an excellent hostess she was. That, however, was likely not the key to Miles's heart.

Myrtle said, "I can't, in good conscience, effect to have a casual visit without letting you know the dreadful news first. Earl Jenkins is dead."

"What?" Martha's hand jerked, and she nearly poured her glass of sweet tea on herself. "But he was just here yesterday, handling my pruning."

Myrtle said, "It only happened this morning. Miles discovered him."

Martha's eyes welled with tears. "Oh, Miles, I'm so sorry you had to find poor Earl. What an awful shock that must have been. Are you doing all right?"

Miles shifted uncomfortably in his seat. He didn't seem to be doing all right at all, but Myrtle figured that had more to do with being at Martha's house than it did finding Earl dead. "It was terrible, yes. At this point, I'm just trying to move forward with my day."

"How brave of you! But what happened? Did he have a heart attack? He was always picking up fast food for lunch, and I warned him that habit of his was going to catch up with him at some point."

Myrtle said, "He was murdered, actually. Bradley's second violent death in less than a week."

Martha seemed quite shaken. Myrtle couldn't decide whether that was because she was shocked by the news, upset at having to find a new landscaper, or because she was stricken with guilt because she was somehow involved.

Myrtle said, "I wanted to warn you that Red will likely be making a trip over to see you, and it won't be a social visit."

Martha put her manicured hand on her chest. "Me? But why would Red want to see me?"

"Well, you know how police investigations are."

"No, I really don't!" protested Martha.

"Red will simply want to speak every suspect he's already spoken with," said Myrtle calmly.

"Me? But Red doesn't think I'm a suspect."

"Doesn't he, dear? Perhaps I was mistaken. It's just that I was there with you when he spoke with you the first time. I have a feeling he'll be dropping by for a follow-up."

Martha was now beginning to look alarmed.

Myrtle dismissively waved her hands in the air. "Don't worry. Just give them your alibi for this morning and things will be hunky-dory."

"But I don't have an alibi this morning. I simply did my usual routine. I got up, rolled out my yoga mat, and stretched. Then I did my daily resistance training with hand weights." Martha batted her eyes at Miles as she played up her general fitness level. Miles shrank back into his chair. "Then I drank my green tea. I followed that by some meditation and journaling. Following that, I went out into the yard and did some more stretching in the sunlight."

Myrtle decided that the next thing on her list could be that she puttered over and killed Earl Jenkins. The detailed retelling of her morning routine made it seem as though she protested too much. She broke in to interrupt Martha's dull monologue.

"You must have known Earl well, since he was your yardman," said Myrtle smoothly. "Did you get along well with him?"

"Oh, Earl wasn't my yardman. Earl just came over every once in a while to prune for me or do other specialty work. I have a gentleman named Dusty who mows for me."

Myrtle's eyebrows shot up to her hairline. "Dusty? You use Dusty?"

"Yes, I think he's a diamond in the rough. He's seemingly so uncouth, but he's actually rather wise, don't you think?"

Myrtle did not. She did wonder how he managed to make Martha's grounds look so lovely. He clearly didn't avoid showing up at her house, as he did Myrtle's.

For the first time since they'd arrived at Martha's house, Miles looked genuinely amused and as if he might be enjoying himself.

"You think he's wise?" asked Myrtle. "Dusty?"

"I do. And so devoted to his craft."

Now Myrtle suspected Dusty was playing up his role for Martha's benefit. "You see, I employ Dusty, and I've had quite a different experience. I find he shirks his duties and is loath to work."

"I can't imagine how you've come to that conclusion, Myrtle," said Martha with a shrug.

Myrtle tilted her head to one side, thoughtfully. "May I inquire how much you're paying Dusty to take care of your lawn?"

Martha listed a sum that was more than double what Myrtle paid him.

"I see," said Myrtle.

Miles added helpfully, "Martha also doesn't have any gnomes to weed-whack around."

"Yes, I know that, Miles," said Myrtle between gritted teeth. "Although right now, I only have my Elvis gnome out there."

Martha and Miles exchanged a look.

"Anyway," said Martha, determined to change the subject from gnomes and yards, "I'm delighted to see you both. I'd wanted to speak with you, Myrtle, about doing something special in memory of Hortense. I was thinking the garden club should create a memorial of some kind. I'm going to ask the ladies to vote on it during the next garden club meeting, so I need you to put your thinking cap on."

Myrtle nodded. "I'll mull over some ideas."

Martha continued as if Myrtle hadn't said anything. "We could establish an annual award at garden club. Tippy is getting a scholarship started for needy gardeners so they wouldn't have to pay dues. Perhaps that could be named after Hortense."

"That would be nice. Our friend Wanda is the recipient of the first scholarship, I believe."

"Yes," said Martha. "We could also extend it in future years to include local students interested in horticulture, botany, or a related field."

Miles was again looking as if a caffeine infusion might be required.

Martha was continuing to mull the issue over. "On the other hand, we could donate a memorial bench to the park with a plaque that honors Hortense's love of gardening."

Myrtle herself was becoming restless now. "Yes. That would be very nice."

Finally, Martha seemed to realize that her guests might want to move on to other things. Martha said, "I'd like to show you some of my art if you're up for a tour. I love to have an audience, but it seems that everyone is so very busy these days that they simply can't come by to visit."

Myrtle and Miles grudgingly acquiesced. Myrtle had the distinct impression that the floral art that Martha was going to show them was, once again, not going to comprise roses and baby's breath like the old-fashioned arrangements she preferred.

Fifteen minutes later, Martha was still talking about her philosophy behind her flower arranging, which had much to do with making soft things, like flowers, look spiky and rather dangerous and unwelcoming. Several of her arrangements were devoid of any bright color at all, which was difficult to manage with flowers.

Myrtle was determined to move on. "Very nice, Martha. Thanks for the tour. I wanted to ask you another question, if I could."

Martha beamed at her. "Oh, I already know what you're going to ask. And the answer is that I'd love to teach you how to make art just like mine. I'm actually going to teach a workshop in another couple of weeks over at the church."

Myrtle's face fell. "Actually, that wasn't quite what I was going to ask. It's about the murders."

"Is it?" Martha looked uncomfortable. "Well, there's not much I can tell you about those."

"I was wondering who you thought might be responsible."

Martha said slowly, "But I told you the last time we talked. I thought Earl Jenkins was responsible for Hortense's death."

Myrtle suspected Martha might be astoundingly dim. Far slower than she'd originally thought. "Yes, but it doesn't seem that way now, does it? Not with Earl dead."

Martha pursed her lips in thought. "Maybe Earl killed Hortense and someone else killed Earl. For revenge." She looked pleased with herself for having come up with this scenario.

"Who might have done that?" asked Myrtle, trying to be patient. She'd always felt as if she'd been a very patient schoolteacher, back in the day. But as she grew older, she felt more and more impatient.

"Why, probably Arthur Wilkins. He was dating Hortense, after all. He likely did the noble thing and defended Hortense's honor."

Myrtle frowned. "That's doesn't make sense. She wasn't dishonored. She was murdered."

Martha was rapidly losing interest in the conversation. "Whatever."

Myrtle took a deep breath to calm herself down. When she spoke, it was in a gently curious voice. "I suppose you'll be the head judge for the flower show? Once it's rescheduled, I mean. That worked out very well for you, didn't it?"

"Hortense's death? In a terrible way, I suppose it did." She made a face. "Except I don't believe I want to judge the rescheduled flower show. I'd rather step in for next year's show. Otherwise, people might talk. I'll find another suitable candidate for the job."

Myrtle said, "I did hear that you were devastated when Hortense made derogatory remarks about your plants."

Martha shrugged. "People get jealous of me sometimes. Maybe someone *wanted* me to be devastated, so that's why they said that. I can't imagine why they're so very envious of me." Martha batted her eyelashes at Miles.

"So it didn't bother you at all when Hortense said awful things about your arrangements?"

"Not a bit," said Martha. "It just helped me realize Hortense didn't have the right disposition to be a flower show judge. If she was going to make people feel small about their entries, she didn't need to be someone who garden club chose to represent them."

Myrtle gave her a smile. "And right you are. Well, I believe Miles and I should be heading along now. Thanks so much for the refreshments and the lovely tour."

As soon as she and Miles were safely in his car, Myrtle muttered, "Lovely tour, my foot."

Miles said, "Oh, I thought you loved the neutral flower arrangements."

"Don't be snarky, Miles." Myrtle sighed. "Martha, for some reason, really gets on my nerves. There's just something about her. She's like a Tippy wannabe, but not nearly as bright or as genuine as Tippy is."

"I'll be delighted if you decide to avoid Martha in the future," said Miles fervently.

"Well, she's definitely sweet on you. I suppose she has good taste in some respects, even if her artistic creations are horrid."

Myrtle's phone rang. "Wanda? How are you?"

Chapter Twelve

As a matter of fact, Wanda didn't sound good at all. "Not great. Gotta do a video call with that rich lady. My phone ain't up to it, though."

"Your phone? You mean the burner phone you've been using? No, I wouldn't think it would support video."

Miles shifted uncomfortably, which usually preceded him offering to purchase something.

Myrtle continued, "But I thought you'd been doing video calls with her earlier."

"On Dan's laptop. But it done broke. Ain't wanting to spend money from my savings. Using that for the used car."

Myrtle said, "Okay, here's what you need to do. You need to let your client, Ms. Moneybags, know that you have some obstacles in the way of providing her with her fortunes. That you have major technical difficulties. Since your sessions with her are so valuable to her, I'm sure she won't think twice about setting you up with a laptop and a reliable internet connection."

Wanda was quiet for a few moments. "Dunno 'bout that." She sounded as if she was in an agony of indecision.

"Believe me, I do."

Wanda hemmed and hawed for a few more moments. Myrtle said, "How about this—give me her phone number, and I'll tell her I'm your agent."

This prompted Miles to raise his eyebrows.

Wanda hesitated a few more moments before reluctantly giving Myrtle the phone number. Myrtle hung up with Wanda and called the out-of-state number.

"Hello?" inquired a genteel and rather bored-sounding voice.

"Hi, this is Myrtle Clover. I'm Wanda's representative. I needed to inform you of some technical difficulties Wanda is experiencing."

The woman on the other end sounded more alert. "Oh, no. I won't be able to speak with Wanda today?"

"I'm afraid not. You see, Wanda lives in a rural area with poor internet and cell connection. She can't afford to get better internet, which is what's needed for streaming and zoom calls. Plus, the laptop she was using for your previous sessions has broken, and she doesn't have the funds to replace it."

The woman sounded alarmed. "But I really wanted to speak with Wanda about an upcoming trip I'm going to take."

"When's your trip?" asked Myrtle.

"In ten days."

Myrtle said, "That's plenty of time for you to order her a new laptop, sent to her address. I can provide you with that information."

The woman fumbled to get something to write with, then jotted down the address. "What about the internet?"

Myrtle said, "If you can pay her internet bill and upgrade her to a higher tier, I'm sure it will resolve the issue."

The woman didn't think twice about it. "Of course. I'll call her and we'll add my bank account to have her service automatically debited from. Thank you."

With that, the phone call was ended. Miles looked impressed. "That actually worked out better than I expected."

Myrtle shrugged. "The woman places a lot of importance in what Wanda has to say. She'll do anything to keep that line of communication going."

"Aren't you going to call Wanda and let her know it's taken care of?"

"I think she probably already knows. It's a bonus of being a psychic."

The rest of Monday was quite relaxing. Myrtle and Miles had a quiet afternoon. Myrtle checked in with Elaine, and she was feeling much improved. Elaine assured Myrtle again that she didn't need to cook for her. Jack was being a splendid boy and spending time coloring and playing with Play-Doh.

The next morning, Myrtle called Miles. "Feel like doing a little investigating?"

"I suppose so."

"You really need to demonstrate some enthusiasm, Miles. Sidekicks should be eager."

Miles said, "I'm not sure that's in a sidekick's job description. It seems to be more of a position where one listens, rarely interjects, and engages in wild speculation with the sleuth later on."

"You're a vital asset, Miles! I'd like you to accompany me on a trip back to the hardware store to see Harold Daniels."

Miles sighed. "What useless thing will I be purchasing this time? Weatherstripping?"

"Don't be silly. We'll be returning your nozzle, of course."

Miles sounded uncomfortable. "What will I say is wrong with it?"

"You'll simply say it doesn't suit. That's easy enough."

Miles said, "I suppose so. I'd like to get the thing off my hands. It's sitting on my coffee table, looking very out of place. You were going to pick up that light bulb, too, weren't you?"

"That's right. So, you see, it's a legitimate errand."

"During which, you'll be interrogating a murder suspect," said Miles.

"Naturally. That's the way it works. Will you be ready in ten minutes?"

Miles was, and they set off for the hardware store. Harold, if possible, was in an even more jovial mood than he'd been during their previous visit.

"How are you two fine citizens? Welcome back to the store! What can I help you with, young man?" said Harold to Miles with a wink. "More nozzles?"

Miles flushed at this and proffered the paper bag that held the nozzle and the receipt. "Actually, I'd like to return this one."

Harold's eyebrows flew up. "Return it? What was wrong with it?"

Miles shifted on his feet. "It just didn't suit."

"You want to try a different type of nozzle? Pistol grip, dial hose, high-pressure? What are you using the nozzle for?"

Miles glanced over at Myrtle. Myrtle said in her sternest tone, "Now, Harold. You offer a money-back guarantee, with *no questions asked*. I've just heard quite a few questions."

Harold gave a guffawing laugh. "You're absolutely right, Miss M, as always. Pardon me, Miles. I'll get that return processed for you straight away. I know what it's like to make an impulse buy."

Miles gave him a tight smile. He was not the type of person to give into impulses, if indeed he experienced impulses at all, which seemed unlikely.

They followed him over to the cash register, passing a couple of toddlers and their mothers looking at baby chicks. A man in fishing gear was buying Nightcrawlers. Myrtle pulled out an RC Cola from a bottle dispenser and purchased it after Miles's return was completed.

Myrtle said casually, "I suppose you heard about Earl Jenkins."

"Who?" asked Harold, looking curious.

"You know him, I'm sure. He's a local landscaper. I'm sure he must have come in here to get his lawnmower blades sharpened and that sort of thing." Myrtle gave a brief description of the man.

Harold nodded. "I think I know who you're talking about. He's been in here from time to time. What about him?"

"He's dead," said Myrtle simply. "Murdered. Miles found him."

Miles looked uncomfortable again, disliking being identified as a person who discovered bodies.

"Is that so?" asked Harold, giving a low whistle. "What is this town coming to? Red must be beside himself trying to get things under control in Bradley. Any word on how the investigation is going?"

Myrtle shook her head. "No. I'm sure he'll be likely heading this way soon, though, to speak with you again. Apparently, Earl's death is related to Hortense's. You can ask Red yourself."

Harold said, "Well, that'll be a brief conversation. I didn't know the guy, so what possible reason would I have to kill him?"

"You have an alibi for yesterday morning? I'm sure Red will ask."

Harold snorted. "Hanging out at the hardware store, as usual. That's when I sharpen tools and make the key copies for the orders that come in. No witnesses, naturally."

"You don't have any security cameras here?" asked Myrtle.

"In Bradley? No. Never have. It would have been handy for giving me an alibi, for sure. But I can't think that anybody but the killer would be concerned about setting up an alibi. Normal, law-abiding folks are too busy with regular life to worry about stuff like that."

"That's very true," said Myrtle sweetly. "And very brave of you, since you don't have one."

Harold smiled at her. "Brave is my middle name. Besides, your boy doesn't have anything on me."

"Hasn't he? Oh, that's good. I must have gotten confused, then."

"Confused about what, Miss Myrtle?"

"I heard a rumor that you'd had quite the heated argument with Hortense just recently."

Harold made a dismissive wave with his hand. "That's the thing about rumors. They're just not true. Whoever it was must have misunderstood what they thought they saw."

"I believe it was what they *heard*. And it was two different people. Are you quite sure you didn't have a conflagration with Hortense?"

Harold said, "If a conflagration is an argument, then I surely didn't. Although Hortense and I would snap at each other sometimes, you know. It was sort of our love language. We never meant anything by it. Like I said before, she and I were still good friends until the end."

Harold was beginning to look as if he might want to escape the conversation. Myrtle shot Miles a look to indicate he should keep Harold interested. Miles cleared his throat. "Do you have any plans for the shop now? I know you'd mentioned last time that you were coming into some money."

Myrtle gave Miles an approving smile. If there was one thing that would keep Harold hooked on their conversation, it was the opportunity to brag.

"Why, yes indeed, I *do* have plans," said Harold. He suddenly started acting very much like Myrtle felt a local squire might behave. "I'm looking to get some more help in the store. That'll free up my time a little. I've spent all day, every day, over here since I can remember. It'll be nice to hire folks to take over some of those duties I've been saddled with."

"What kinds of things are you hoping to do in your free time?" asked Miles politely.

Harold chuckled. "Do you know, I don't have the faintest idea? You're retired, aren't you?"

Miles nodded.

"What do you find to do with yourself all the long hours of the day?" asked Harold.

Miles gave Myrtle something of a reproachful look, as if she took up far more of those hours than he wanted.

Myrtle answered for Miles. "He does lots of things. He works on sudoku and crossword puzzles, plays chess, and watches TV."

Harold didn't seem particularly interested in these pastimes. "Gotcha," he said. But he was already looking around the hardware store for something else to occupy him.

"Maybe traveling would be more up your alley," suggested Myrtle.

Harold brightened at this. "You're right. I'd love to go to see Europe and other places. Take a boat down the Thames to see the Eiffel Tower."

Myrtle kindly didn't point out that Harold would be hard-pressed to see the French landmark from London.

Harold continued, "See, the way I look at it is that Hortense actually did me a huge favor by divorcing me. Now I can do these things on my own. I can come up with my own itinerary, full of the things that *I* want to see and do. I won't have to take anyone else into account." Harold looked delighted at this prospect.

"Going back to poor Hortense, the last time we spoke, you thought Emily White, who'd taken some plants from Hortense, might have been involved. Do you still feel that way?"

Harold shrugged. "Well, sure. *She's* not dead, is she? She could have done it."

"How mad, exactly, was Hortense over the plants?"

"I heard she was plenty mad. Furious. Even though she and Emily had a lot in common."

Myrtle asked, "Did they? I wouldn't have said that was the case."

"Hortense didn't start out her life with a ton of money, either. And she loved plants just as much as Emily. I wouldn't have been surprised to learn that Hortense swiped a plant or two when she was young. But those were some prize-winning plants. Hortense was hugely protective over the plants and flowers in her garden . . . especially the ones that gave her ribbons."

Myrtle decided to shake things up a little. "I understand you were at the flower show when poor Hortense perished."

Harold colored. "Someone is lying," he said, furious. His genial manner fell completely away. In that moment, it was easier to picture him angry enough to kill.

Myrtle shrugged. "Would it have been the end of the world if you were there? As long as you didn't murder Hortense, you'd still be in the clear."

"I had a completely cordial relationship with Hortense. Why would I kill her?"

Myrtle thought that inheriting enough money to travel the world seemed like an excellent reason.

A man approached the cash register, wanting to pay for his new garden hose.

"Good seeing you fine people," said Harold with his salesman grin back firmly in place.

Miles and Myrtle walked out. "I'm not sure that was very illuminating," said Miles.

"He could have been more helpful," said Myrtle. "It's all very irritating how these suspects continue to hoard their secrets. If they'd just cough them up, this case would be over in no time."

"You can't blame them for not wanting to go to jail," said Miles mildly.

"Of course I can. If they'd wanted to avoid jail, they shouldn't have committed two murders to begin with."

They got into the car, and Miles drove back to Myrtle's house. He made a few attempts at small talk, but Myrtle didn't engage, instead giving vague answers that proved she wasn't listening whatsoever.

Back in Myrtle's house, Miles took a seat on the sofa, and Myrtle plopped down in her armchair.

"You forgot that light bulb again," said Miles.

"Oh, pooh. I knew there was something I'd forgotten. Oh well. That'll give me an excuse for next time."

Miles prompted, "Bring me up to speed again on where everything stands in this case. I think it's time for something of a review."

Chapter Thirteen

Myrtle brightened. "Indeed it is, Miles. A wrap-up. Very well. To start with, we have Martha Green. She was generally unhappy with Hortense because Hortense was the head judge of the flower show. She was *very* unhappy about all the unkind things Hortense has said about her flowers."

Miles gave a shudder. "Well-deserved, in my opinion. Why make flowers ugly? What's the purpose of that?"

"To get attention, I suppose."

"Does Martha lack attention in her life?" asked Miles.

"She must think so. It appears she's always trying to get it. Anyway, she takes a lot of pride in these monstrosities she creates, and it hurt her feelings that Hortense was mean about them. Plus, she was on the scene."

"Martha the murderer," said Miles, as if trying it out on his tongue. "Somehow, I just can't picture it."

"That's showing an astounding lack of imagination, Miles. I can see it all quite easily. Martha would be trailing Hortense around, perhaps. Trying to get a handle on how she was judging the arrangements exhibit. Hovering. Then Hortense swings around. Her mouth twists cruelly. She says something horrid to Martha. Martha is momentarily blinded by tears, but blinks them away as Hortense resumes critiquing the flower exhibit. Martha picks up the clay flowerpot and swings it with all her might directly at Hortense's head."

Miles said dryly, "Very vivid."

"Isn't it? Mind you, I'm not completely convinced that Martha is our perpetrator. We also have Emily, who is someone else we need to interview again. Emily came from a somewhat impoverished background. She adores nature and gardening and has a true passion for developing her own collection of flora and fauna. However, she can't afford the beautiful things she wants to grow in her own yard."

Miles said, "Emily discovers Hortense has a beautiful and well-stocked garden. She asks Hortense if she can divide her Hostas and giant fern."

"Or maybe she didn't. It's all very unclear. At any rate, Emily goes over to Hortense's to collect her divided plants. Hortense spots her and, very unhappy, tells Emily off. She threatens prosecution. And she tells people about it. Which," said Myrtle, "leads us to Earl Jenkins."

"The deceased Earl Jenkins," reminds Miles.

"True. But I'm mentioning Earl mainly because I'm seeing a pattern in the way Hortense treated others. She seemed to have been very fond of reprimanding people, then telling others about their misdeeds. Hortense might have threatened legal action against Emily, which is certainly a motive for Emily to have murdered her. And Hortense made it challenging for Earl to find other work when she spread the word that he'd used weed-killer on her prize roses."

Miles said, "But then we have Harold, Hortense's ex-husband. She wasn't unkind to him at all. She apparently left him a good deal of money."

"It appears she did. I can only imagine that Hortense just didn't see the rush in changing her will after her divorce from Harold. But I'm not at all convinced that Hortense wasn't unkind to him. I have the feeling their relationship was a lot more fractious than Harold wants to make out."

"I suppose the money itself would be quite a motive," said Miles. "Assuming Harold knew about the will and that Hortense hadn't changed it." He paused. "Who else do we have?"

"Arthur, our friendly neighborhood botanist."

"And Hortense's ex-boyfriend," added Miles.

"Correct. Our friend Arthur apparently had something of a rocky breakup with Hortense. It appears to me that he felt snubbed. We know Hortense was a straight-shooter, and she may not have held her punches when she broke up with Arthur. Could Arthur have nursed that resentment and let it all bubble over when he attended the flower show?"

"He says he wasn't at the flower show," noted Miles.

"Yes, but you know how it is with these suspects. You can't believe a single word they say. I find it hard to believe that Arthur would skip something like a flower show to do some sort of boring administrative work."

Miles, always a stickler for getting facts straight, said, "I believe it was research of some sort. A request from a state agency."

"Whatever. That doesn't sound more interesting than hopping in the car and seeing an immaculate collection of various plants."

Miles said, "So, to recap, the suspects are all lying."

"That's right, Miles. As per usual."

Myrtle tapped the arm of her chair with her fingers. "It feels like something is missing."

"One of the suspects?" Miles seemed to count them up in his head. "I believe you covered everyone. Earl used to be a suspect for Hortense's death, but he's out of the running now."

"Not a suspect. Something else." She snapped her fingers. "I know. A funeral. Usually we have a funeral by this point. It functions as an opportunity for us to see at least some suspects."

"I thought it was an opportunity for the deceased to be interred," said Miles dryly.

"Yes, but that's not the part that's useful for us, is it? Ordinarily, someone is holding a memorial service or a funeral right about now. I go to put on my funeral outfit and find that it somehow is covered by remnants of the food at the last funeral reception."

"I believe we've talked about the need for a spare funeral outfit. Especially in this town," said Miles. "Funerals are quite persistent events here."

"Spare funeral outfits cost money, Miles. I don't think I should be expected to have a large funeral wardrobe, despite the town's high death rate. Anyway, back to the funerals. Red is always there, looking for telltale signs of guilt or smugness from the attendees. You and I navigate the daunting church ladies who serve us delicious artery-clogging Southern foods from a buffet. Then we speak with a suspect or two and start figuring out who the murderer is. But there hasn't been one. Or even a mention of one."

Miles asked, "Did Hortense have children?"

"No children."

Miles said, "And she was divorced. No husband."

"Correct. Although don't you think Harold Daniels could put together something? After all, it sounds as if she left a significant amount of money to him."

Miles shrugged. "Perhaps he's not interested in doing the right thing. Maybe he's convinced himself that Hortense wouldn't have liked a ceremony."

"I'm going to give Tippy a call. She'll know if there are plans to commemorate Hortense's life in any way."

"Don't you mean *celebrate* her life?" asked Miles.

"I don't think anyone would do that, do you?" Myrtle pulled out her phone. "Tippy? Myrtle Clover. I was just thinking about Hortense Winston. Yes. I wondered if you knew anything about a funeral or a memorial service for her." Myrtle listened for a few moments as Tippy spoke. "I see. All right, then. No, I was just curious. Your plans sound completely appropriate, yes. See you soon." Myrtle hung up.

Miles lifted an eyebrow. "I heard plans being mentioned."

"Oh, just for garden club. We're to have a moment of silence or something. And there's to be a memorial bench or some such. But there's no funeral in the works."

Miles said, "What about Earl? Did he have any family?"

"His parents are long dead. I do remember he had a brother growing up. I'm not sure where he is living now. I'm sure Red must have informed him of Earl's death. Perhaps there'll be a funeral down the road for him."

"So no funerals in the near future. Keeping that in mind, what's our next step?" asked Miles.

"I have some non-case-related things to work on, actually. I want to check on Elaine and perhaps give her a break for a couple of hours this afternoon."

"I thought you mentioned earlier that she was doing better," said Miles.

"That was last night. You know how these pulled muscles can be. Plus, I should write that story on Earl's death for the paper. Otherwise, Sloan will let some other reporter scoop it, and that will completely infuriate me. And, in other matters, I believe I should get Puddin out here. The floor badly needs vacuuming. Do you have plans for tomorrow?"

"I have chess club. I probably should spend a bit more time practicing on the computer."

"But you did well during the tournament," said Myrtle. "It seems you might have plenty of practice in."

"Yes, but now I've set expectations high. Now people will *expect* me to win."

"It doesn't seem like such a terrible situation to be in. But if practice makes you feel more confident, that's the way to go." Myrtle pulled out her phone. "I suppose I should go ahead and call Puddin. It'll take forever to persuade her to come and clean my house."

Miles took his leave as Myrtle called Puddin.

Dusty answered the phone. He howled for Puddin, then hastily handed the phone over before Myrtle could ask him when he was going to mow her grass.

"I already know," said Puddin sullenly.

"That I need you to come clean my house? I'd imagine that would be obvious, since I don't make social phone calls with you."

"Maybe next week," said Puddin.

"Today. I need you to come right now. I suspect you didn't vacuum last time you were here."

Puddin muttered. "It's a lie. I did vacuum."

"Then you did an awful job at it. Regardless, I need a do-over."

Puddin muttered some more. But the mutterings seemed to indicate that she might acquiesce to coming by.

Myrtle then hopped onto the computer and quickly penned an excellent article about Earl Jenkins death. She sent it to Sloan with the pointed subject: *for tomorrow's front page.*

Then it was time to check on Elaine. Although Elaine assured Myrtle she was feeling better, she sounded relieved at the idea of Myrtle collecting Jack for a little while.

"You're sure it won't be any trouble?" asked Elaine.

"Trouble? My darling grandson? Of course not! It's my pleasure. We'll have a big time."

Jack seemed delighted to see his grandmother when she tapped at the door minutes later. "We'll play!" he said.

"Yes, we will. We'll play, have snacks, and then watch cartoons when we get tired. So much fun."

And it was. Myrtle and Jack made forts from sheets and beach towels and basically destroyed the house. Then they had a picnic of peanut butter and graham crackers on the living room floor. It was marvelous.

Marvelous until Myrtle realized she'd spent far too much time on the floor. Her joints protested when she tried to rise. "Pooh. It looks like I'm stuck, Jack."

Jack, a very gallant two-year-old, attempted to pull Myrtle off the floor. This attempt was unsuccessful.

"Can you find Nana's cane? I believe it might be in one of the forts."

Jack scurried off to look in all the different forts they'd constructed. Finally, he came back, bearing the cane, which was taller than he was, in his hands like a trophy.

With the help of the cane and with Jack cheering her on, Myrtle could propel herself off the floor. It was just in time for a knock on the door.

"That must be Puddin," said Myrtle. "I'll need to chat with her for a minute. Do you want to watch a little TV?"

Jack was looking a wee bit sleepy after the afternoon adventures. Myrtle quickly found a cartoon and then hurried to the door. "Coming!" she called out.

But she'd made a fatal error in not checking to see whom was on her doorstep. It was her detestable neighbor Erma out there instead of Puddin.

Myrtle drew back instinctively as Erma leaned toward her. Erma was wearing a particularly horrid and loud outfit.

Erma brayed in laughter. "I see you've noticed my new clothes. Fashionable, aren't they?"

"I don't know much about fashion," prevaricated Myrtle. She devoutly hoped that Erma would disappear, especially if Myrtle didn't provide her with much conversational fuel.

"No, I guess you wouldn't. Since Tippy complimented me at the flower show, I've been working on making cool updates to my wardrobe. Like these clothes."

Myrtle gritted her teeth.

Erma pushed her way in a bit and stared. "Did you have a burglar come in?"

"What? Oh, no. Jack and I made forts. It was a lot of fun."

"If you say so," said Erma doubtfully. She gave a hideous smile at Jack. "Hi, Jack!"

Jack was sleepily engrossed in the cartoon, but rallied enough to beam at Erma and wave his hand politely.

Myrtle said pointedly, "I really need to get back to Jack."

"I just needed to tell you one thing, Myrtle. I'm going out of town for a little while. I wanted to let you know so that you could keep an eye on the house for me."

Myrtle beamed at her. "Why, of *course* I will. How long will you be gone?" It was like an answer to a prayer.

"Ten days. I'm going on a really fabulous trip."

Myrtle greatly feared that Erma was going to go into excruciating detail about the trip's particulars. She hurriedly said, "You'll have to tell me about it when you get back. I'll watch the house for you. Now toodle-oo!" With that, Myrtle firmly closed the door and joined Jack in front of the cartoon.

When the doorbell rang ten minutes later, Myrtle cautiously looked outside to make sure there wouldn't be another Erma encounter. This time, though, it was Puddin's sour features that greeted her.

Myrtle opened the door. "Come in, come in. I thought you'd never get here."

Puddin slouched inside and then came to a complete stop. She gaped at Myrtle's living room. "What happened?"

"What? Oh, the forts. Jack and I have been playing."

"I ain't cleanin' that up," said Puddin stoutly.

Myrtle shot her a look. "I can't imagine why I thought a housekeeper would actually *clean*."

"Ain't cleanin' no forts."

"All right, then. You start working in the kitchen while Jack and I put the forts away. Then you can run the vacuum."

Puddin didn't seem delighted with this idea either, but stomped off to the kitchen. She proceeded to pull Myrtle's cleaning supplies out from under the sink to clean up the counters and cabinets. Myrtle said, "And where are *your* supplies, Puddin? You know you're not supposed to be using mine."

Puddin pushed a lank, blonde strand of hair from her pale face. "Ain't got none. Dusty ain't taken me to the store."

"I'll have to have a word with Dusty," said Myrtle. Then, "Come on, Jack. Let's see how fast we can put the forts away." She managed to find a lively timer on her phone that had energetic music. They quickly scrambled around, pulling down blankets and beach towels, folding them up, and putting them away.

"Let's go play outside while Puddin vacuums."

"I'm cleanin' the kitchen," said Puddin sourly.

"Leave the kitchen and vacuum so Jack and I can come back to the living room once we get bored outside."

Puddin gave a beleaguered sigh as Jack and Myrtle headed outside with a collection of Jack's trucks that Myrtle kept in a basket in her closet. They drove the trucks around and about. Myrtle's truck had superpowers since she was driving it on the garden bench where she was sitting. She figured her body was telling her she shouldn't be sitting on the ground any more that day.

Chapter Fourteen

The vacuum turned off and Myrtle and Jack walked back in. Jack wanted to play Memory.

"Great game, Jack," said Myrtle. "And one that I consistently lose when I play you."

Jack gave her a big grin. Then he looked thoughtfully at Puddin. "Can you play, too?"

Puddin's eyes narrowed at the little boy. "Yer Nana says I gotta clean."

"You could take a short break, Puddin. Before you finish cleaning the kitchen."

Puddin grumbled a bit as Myrtle set up the game at the kitchen table. Jack watched attentively as Myrtle placed the little cardboard cards in rows on the table. Puddin eyed the cards suspiciously.

"Now, Jack and I know the rules, but I'll fill you in, Puddin. When it's your turn, you'll turn over two cards. If they match, you may go again. If they don't match, you'll turn them back over again. You'll want to try to remember the cards that the other players turn over. The player with the most pairs wins."

Puddin listened carefully, her beady eyes narrowed. "Got it."

Puddin was allowed to go first, since she was new at the game. She picked up her two cards, shielding them from Jack and Myrtle's view.

"No, no, Puddin! That's against the rules," said Myrtle sternly.

Jack chortled. "No, no, Puddin!"

Puddin glowered at them both. "Didn't say that was against the rules."

"I thought that would be inferred, since the players are supposed to remember the cards the others uncover," said Myrtle. "Try again."

Puddin reluctantly showed the two cards to the others. They weren't a match, so she turned them back over again.

Although Myrtle had an excellent memory for names, faces, and books she'd read, her performance when playing Memory was decidedly subpar. She had a single match to her name as Jack and Puddin battled it out.

Jack's small forehead was creased in concentration as he uncovered cards. Puddin was hunched over the kitchen table, looking very tense.

"I'll just remind you both that Memory isn't a case of life or death," said Myrtle.

Puddin glared at her for interjecting and distracting her from her focus on the game.

"You could l-e-t him w-i-n," said Myrtle.

"Nope," said Puddin.

Myrtle decided she shouldn't have been surprised. Puddin was just as childish as Jack, if not more so.

At the end, they counted their pairs to find that Jack had won by two cards.

"Well done, Jack!" said Myrtle, applauding. "My brilliant grandson has done it again."

"Winner is the best two out of three," declared Puddin, turning the cards back over again to play another game.

"No, it's time to put the game away. I need to return Jack to his mother, and you need to finish cleaning my house."

"The kitchen," corrected Puddin.

"The kitchen first. Then the rest of the house. That's the way it works."

Puddin ambled away, muttering what sounded like dire threats as she left.

Elaine seemed better-rested when Myrtle brought Jack home. "Did you have fun?" Elaine asked Jack.

"Yes! Played trucks, forts, and Memory."

"Did you?" Elaine gave Myrtle a rueful look. "It sounds like your house might have gotten wrecked in the process."

"Oh, it was my *pleasure*. Besides, Puddin is over there now. She'll put everything back to rights."

Elaine said, "I'm surprised Puddin didn't boycott cleaning."

"She wasn't happy about the forts, but she appeared to take everything else in stride," said Myrtle with a shrug.

"Puddin cheats," said Jack solemnly.

"Indeed she does," said Myrtle. "But you ended up beating her anyway, didn't you? That's because cheaters never win."

The rest of the day was quite tranquil. Myrtle followed up with Sloan to make absolutely sure her story about Earl's demise would be on the front page. He spluttered a lot, mentioned dire threats from Red, and seemed very on-the-fence. So Myrtle, not feeling at all reassured, got up the following morning and trudged out to get her paper from the front yard, where it had landed next to her Elvis gnome. She was relieved to see that her article was front and center on the very front page.

Myrtle then set about calling Miles. She was sure he'd be up, since insomnia usually made him rise long before five a.m. However, he sounded very sleepy and confused when he picked up the phone.

"What? Are you okay, Myrtle?"

"Of course I am. Are *you* okay? Because you sound decidedly groggy."

Miles sighed. "I'm okay. I was merely sleeping."

"Are you certain you were sleeping? You sound as if you've broken out of a coma."

"You know how rare good sleep is. I'm going to get back to it," he said in a pointed manner.

"Oh, that's a pity. I was thinking we could have an early breakfast at the diner this morning. Before your chess club. Perhaps we could find out what Emily White thought of Earl's death."

Miles yawned. "We could do an early lunch there. Breakfast is out of the question right now."

Myrtle told him she'd talk to him later and hung up the phone. She didn't feel at all like waiting until lunchtime. But she also didn't feel like walking in the dark to the diner. Perhaps she'd wait until a later hour, like ten o'clock, and use the time to run errands and pop quickly into the diner. They'd still be serving breakfast then, and the lunch crowd wouldn't have arrived yet.

Her planning done, Myrtle opened the newspaper. She quickly noticed that her story was the only one that didn't have a single typo. Myrtle took out her red pen, the one she had close at hand when she read the newspaper. She carefully underlined all the mistakes she saw, writing notes in the margins occasionally. She decided she'd bring the newspaper with her when she was downtown later on and leave it with Sloan. Myrtle was sure he didn't want a paper full of errors, and her markings would remind him to proofread.

After she'd finished the crossword and the sudoku, she heard a meowing from outside her kitchen window.

"Darling Pasha!" she said. She let the black cat in and fed her. Pasha ate hungrily. "Not decimating nature as much, then?" asked Myrtle. "I'd think you wouldn't be as hungry if you were consuming small rodents and birds."

Pasha looked up at her as if she disputed that claim, then continued eliminating the cat food as quickly as she could.

"Perhaps I should pick up more cat food at the Piggly Wiggly as one of my assorted errands," mused Myrtle.

Pasha's expression appeared to agree with her.

"What's today?" Myrtle peered at the newspaper to see what date it was. "Excellent! I should have money in my bank account now."

She decided she'd better check to make sure her retirement check had hit her account. It certainly wouldn't do to find out at the grocery store or the diner that she had no money. Myrtle got on her computer to take a look. Fortunately, she was positively flush with cash. In retired teacher terms, at least.

"We're rich, Pasha!" said Myrtle.

Pasha beamed at her. She then started assiduously bathing herself, since she was finished eating.

Myrtle, realizing she needed to kill time, decided scrolling online was better than the pre-dawn television offerings. She started reading the news, then quickly stopped reading the news. "Too much craziness," she muttered.

Pasha leaped into her lap and curled up into a ball. Myrtle absently stroked her while she moved on to social media. Although she rarely updated her own accounts, she rather enjoyed seeing what everyone else was doing. From what she saw in her feed, they all seemed to be going on exotic vacations with their brilliant offspring. She was deluged by images of crystal-clear turquoise waters lapped up on impossibly clean beaches, picturesque sunsets, and superhuman grandchildren.

"The reality is," said Myrtle to Pasha, "that they're likely squabbling with those children and grandchildren when the camera isn't on them. They're having to wait in long lines in the heat to see the attractions they're taking pictures of. It's never as much fun as it all appears."

Pasha gave her a knowing feline smile.

Soon, it was nearly ten o'clock. Myrtle readied herself to go downtown. She knew she wanted to go to the store, the diner, and the newspaper office. Perhaps she could manage a trip to the library, too. She was definitely not going to check out the book club's latest read, however. It was some sort of soppy junk that didn't sound at all interesting. She was rather in the mood to read something scary. Perhaps *The Haunting of Hill House* would be available. Shirley Jackson knew how to write.

When Myrtle opened the front door, Pasha scampered away in another direction, perhaps motivated by the movement of something very small and furry in Erma's yard. Myrtle smiled. It would be nice if Pasha could take on all the assorted wildlife in Erma's yard before Erma returned from her trip. It was a pity that she wasn't big enough to eliminate the deer that had gnawed on Myrtle's prize roses.

Myrtle set off for downtown. There was a light breeze outside and shade under the trees that lined both sides of the road. Myrtle headed first to the *Bradley Bugle*'s office. It was housed in a quaint, weathered building that had seen better days. The moment she stepped inside, she was greeted by the distinct aroma of ink, paper, and musty books. The lighting, as always in the newsroom, was very dim, and Myrtle had to take a few moments to adjust after coming in from the sunny outdoors. Every corner and flat space was covered by labyrinthine stacks of newspapers, photographs, and documents. This was a newspaper where everyone's tale eventually found its place in print.

Sloan spoke before Myrtle could make him out in the shady room. "Miss Myrtle!" he said, sounding alarmed, which was his usual reaction to her unexpected appearances.

Her eyes finally adjusted, and she spotted Sloan across the room. Myrtle picked her way over to him. "I've got something for you."

"Not another story," said Sloan. "There wasn't another murder, was there?"

"Not yet, no. And, if I have anything to do with it, there won't be one at all." She fished the newspaper out of her large purse, waving it at Sloan. "I brought you a corrected version of the paper for your perusal."

"Oh." Sloan looked less than excited to be the recipient of the newspaper, which fairly bled red ink.

"I figured it might help you out the next time around. Live and learn, right?"

"Yes, Miss Myrtle," said Sloan. He sadly took the newspaper from her. Then he asked, "Do you have a helpful hints column ready for me? I know we talked about it last time."

"*You* talked about it last time. However, it so happens that I do have a few tips that were sent in from my readers." Myrtle dove into her massive purse again, rustling around until she found the piece of paper she'd jotted on. "Let's see. Maribelle Maples says if you accidentally over-salt a dish, place an ice cube into the pot. The excess salt sticks to the ice, making it easier to scoop out."

Sloan said, "Wow, that's pretty amazing. I bet our readers will love that. Is it legitimate?"

Myrtle gave him a stern look. "You know I'm not the helpful hints fact-checker, Sloan. That's more of an editor's job. Perhaps you should call Maribelle and ask her. Or over-salt a soup and try it out."

Sloan nodded. He typed the hint into a file on his computer.

Myrtle continued, "Tanya Wheeler said that you can un-stick zippers by rubbing pencils on them."

Sloan considered this. "The eraser end or the pointed end?"

"She mentions graphite, so it seems to be the pointed end. And I have no idea if it works," said Myrtle grimly, before Sloan could ask again.

"Right. Was there another one?"

Myrtle said, "Tiny texted me that if you put saucers with beer into your garden, you'll keep snails out of your plants." She paused. "I'd guess that's legitimate. I don't see Tiny wasting beer on something that doesn't work." The inaccurately named Tiny was six foot seven, three-hundred pounds, and an experienced beer consumer.

"Got it," said Sloan, sticking out his tongue as he quickly typed up the copy.

"That's it," said Myrtle. "And now I'd best be on my way. I have a couple of different errands to run."

Sloan's face creased with relief. "Okay, Miss Myrtle. Thanks for the helpful hints. And, uh, the corrected newspaper."

Myrtle breezily waved her hand. "No problem at all; it's my pleasure. One more thing, Sloan."

Sloan froze.

"It's just that you often have your finger on the pulse of Bradley," said Myrtle. "That comes part and parcel with publishing a newspaper, of course. I was wondering what you might know about the potential suspects for the murders of Hortense and Earl."

Sloan now looked panicked. The last thing he wanted was to help Myrtle in any sort of investigating. "I don't know anything. You actually know much more than I do, I'm sure. And Red, of course."

"Yes, but I certainly can't ask Red anything. He's completely impossible." Myrtle stopped talking and just stared at Sloan. She knew from the past that Sloan couldn't handle uncomfortable silences and would jump in to fill them.

Sure enough, only a few moments had gone by before Sloan said nervously, "If you gave me a suspect's name, I could do my best, Miss Myrtle. But I might not have any actual information, just my opinion."

Myrtle rarely put a lot of stock in Sloan's personal opinions, however she felt as if he might be helpful in this particular instance. "How about Harold Daniels?"

Sloan relaxed a bit. "Harold? He's a great guy. He's one of the regulars over at the bar down the street." He suddenly colored as if he were sixteen and in English class and admitting his drinking to his teacher.

"Is he? Has he said much about Hortense's untimely demise?"

Sloan shook his head. "No, but he's talked a lot about the money he's going to be getting."

Myrtle said, "He's really counting his chickens before they hatch. It seems he *will* be getting money, but the probate process isn't exactly speedy."

"No, it's not. Except it turned out that Harold was the beneficiary of Hortense's life insurance policy, her 401K, and some other accounts. Harold says that kind of stuff doesn't have to go through probate. He'll be coming into the money really soon. He even bought us all a round." The memory made Sloan smile fondly.

"I didn't realize there was a life insurance policy. That's very helpful information to have, Sloan."

Sloan beamed, looking as if he expected a gold star.

"How about Emily?"

"Emily?" asked Sloan hesitantly.

"Emily White. She's a young woman who works at Bo's Diner."

Sloan said slowly, "Is she the one who's always getting orders wrong and dropping things on the floor?"

"That would be Emily."

Sloan shook his head. "Don't know her, Miss Myrtle."

Sloan also didn't know Earl well (Sloan maintained his own yard, however poorly), nor Arthur. But he brightened again at the mention of Martha Green. "Yes, I know Martha. She comes into the newsroom from time to time."

"Does she?" asked Myrtle in surprise. "To visit you?"

Sloan colored again. "They're not social visits. She's always here to share information. She was my point of contact for the flower show." He hesitated before saying, "Actually, Miss Myrtle, it was a good thing I had you over at the show. I know Red doesn't like you reporting on crime stories, but even if Hortense hadn't died, I should have had a reporter out at the show. It was an oversight on my part."

"So you'd have had me reporting on the winning exhibits if there hadn't been a murder there," said Myrtle. She wasn't sure whether she felt pleased or irritated by this.

"Yep," said Sloan cheerfully. "Of course, you always write a good story. I really dropped the ball when I didn't have coverage out at the flower show. With Martha haranguing me all the time about the event, you'd think I'd have remembered. But I was out late that Friday night and then the next morning I was getting ready to watch a full day of football."

Myrtle said, "Tell me what you make of Martha."

Sloan said, "She's a hard person to warm to, you know? I'm always worried that I'm somehow going to end up offending Martha. She'll bring in photos of her flower arrangements and insist they need to make it into the paper."

Myrtle made a face. "Yes, I've seen them in there from time to time. And some of her vegetables as well."

"That's right. She'll always bring in her nicest selection of veggies in the summer for me to photograph and put in the paper."

Myrtle said, "It's odd that she brings in photos of her arrangements and then the actual vegetables for you to take photos of."

Sloan shrugged. "She's picky about how she wants her flower arrangements to look. Martha wants the lighting just so. I guess she doesn't care as much about the veggies. It would be nice if she gave me one or two of them, though."

"She leaves with them?" asked Myrtle, raising her eyebrows.

"Sure does. Doesn't even leave a tomato behind." Sloan looked wistful.

Myrtle said, "When she's been here, has she ever said anything about Hortense?"

Sloan snorted. "Boy, has she. It took a while for her to open up, but once she did, she couldn't stop talking about her. Especially lately." Myrtle gave him a prompting look and Sloan continued. "She was furious that Hortense got to be the grand judge this year. She said that Hortense didn't need a bigger head than she already had. They'd apparently been at each other's throats for a while."

"For what reason?"

"Just mutual dislike, from what I could tell." Sloan looked thoughtful for a moment. "Except there was this thing that happened. I don't listen *too* closely when Martha comes in, I have to admit. But do you remember when that celebrity chef came down here to make an episode for his TV show?"

Myrtle said, "I do remember. It was in the paper every single day, as I recall. Where he'd been spotted, where he'd eaten, what he was wearing." Myrtle had found it all most irritating at the time.

"Well, there was that special charity auction, do you remember?"

Myrtle said, "Yes, I have an excellent memory, Sloan. I didn't attend the auction, but I read about it."

"Martha really loved this chef. She watched his TV show all the time. Sometimes she cooked his recipes; she took pictures of those, too, and brought them in."

"Of course she did," said Myrtle, rolling her eyes a bit. Perhaps she should take pictures of her own creations. Martha was getting entirely too much ink in the *Bradley Bugle*.

"Anyway, Martha was so excited to bid for the chance to be part of his studio audience. The winning bid would get free tickets to LA to be part of the show, a tour afterward, and even a private cooking lesson. But then Hortense was determined to win it instead of Martha."

Myrtle could see where this was going. "I'm gathering that it wasn't a silent auction."

"Nope. It was a regular auction where you have to signal to the auctioneer that you're making a bid."

"I'm guessing Hortense won," said Myrtle dryly.

"She did. And Martha was furious."

Myrtle said, "It was rather silly for Martha to be so mad, wasn't it? After all, Hortense might have been a huge fan of the chef, too. It sounds as if Hortense won, fair and square."

"Here's the thing, Miss Myrtle. Martha said Hortense told Tippy that she didn't even know who the chef was. Hortense wasn't one to watch TV. She wasn't into food, either. She merely did it so that Martha wouldn't be able to go."

"Hmm," said Myrtle. "Martha seemed angry enough at Hortense merely because she'd said mean things about Martha's arrangements and because she was the grand judge. The auction might have pushed her over the edge."

At that moment, Maude Meadowlark came into the newsroom, blinking as she adjusted to the dim lighting. "Sloan?" she called out in her tinny voice.

Myrtle sighed. It looked as if her conversation with Sloan was drawing to a close.

"Miss Meadowlark?" asked Sloan, standing courteously. "I'm over here."

Maude came in, her lavender hair adorned with an assortment of vibrant hairpins and flower-shaped barrettes. "I wanted to give you a scoop. I've recently completed my vintage button collection, and I knew the paper would want to cover it. Oh, hi Myrtle."

Myrtle bared her teeth in a grin. She jumped back as a small creature erupted from her large, sequined purse and started barking at her.

"Frou-frou," scolded Maude lovingly.

"See you later, Sloan," said Myrtle as she hurried to the door.

Once back outside, Myrtle considered her options. She figured she should go to the diner next, otherwise she'd be lugging cat food cans and library books with her into the restaurant. But before she could cross the street to the diner, she saw Emily White trudging down the street in what seemed like very dressy clothing.

Myrtle waved at her, and Emily grinned as she walked up. "Miss Myrtle! How are you this beautiful morning?"

"Oh, doing well, I suppose. I was thinking you might be working at the diner this morning."

Emily shook her head. "Not anymore." She showed Myrtle the stack of papers she was carrying. They appeared to be resumes.

"Oh dear," said Myrtle. "Did you decide to leave Bo's Diner?"

"Bo's Diner decided to leave *me*," said Emily with a grin. She sounded remarkably unconcerned about getting fired. "I'm job hunting right now.

Considering how much help the diner needed, getting fired from it seemed like quite an achievement.

Emily brightened. "Say, you don't need any work done around the house, do you? I'm open to all types of employment. I'm mostly focusing on retail establishments downtown, but I'd be happy to work other jobs. I could clean or do errands for you. You don't seem like you drive anymore."

Myrtle swiftly embarked on a dazzling daydream in which her house sparkled and her life was Puddin-free. But then reality came crashing down, as it always did. She couldn't afford to alienate Dusty by firing Puddin. He was the only decent yard-man she could afford. And, if she employed Emily, Emily would either be too costly or perhaps too inept. Puddin, at least, knew *how* to clean. Her problem was simply that she was lazy. Emily, however, had been fired from her job at the diner, which was a feat in itself.

"I'm afraid I already have household help. But I'll keep my ears open and let you know if I hear of anything," said Myrtle.

Emily looked crestfallen. "Got it. Thanks, Miss Myrtle."

"Do you have time for a coffee? My treat."

Emily perked back up again. "Sure, that would be great. I'd like to get off my feet for a few minutes." She held out the afore-mentioned feet and showed Myrtle her high heels.

Myrtle winced. "Yes, let's give you a few minutes of rest." Going to the diner was clearly out, but there was a small coffee-house a few doors down from where they were standing. Myrtle ordered a small coffee. "Get whatever you want, dear," prompt-ed Myrtle as Emily seemed to hesitate.

Emily gave her a grateful look and then ordered. "I'd like a Venti, non-fat, caramel macchiato with almond milk, two pumps of vanilla syrup, one pump of hazelnut syrup, and a smidge of honey drizzle on top. In a to-go cup, please."

Myrtle blinked. She wasn't entirely sure what Emily had ordered. But then, the younger generation often had the ability to befuddle. The barista seemed to take it all in stride.

Myrtle's coffee came out right away. While they were waiting for Emily's, Myrtle decided to broach the subject of Earl. She chose what she hoped was an innocuous, gossipy tone. "Did you know Earl Jenkins at all, dear?"

"Earl? Sure I do. He's sort of like a dad figure to me. He talks to me about plants and even gives me freebies from his yard."

Myrtle was a bit concerned about Emily's use of the present tense when referring to Earl. She very much hoped Emily wouldn't start crying. Myrtle felt quite unprepared to handle crying that morning. "You haven't heard the news, then?"

Chapter Fifteen

E mily's eyes opened wide. "What? Did something happen to Earl? Is he in the hospital?"

"I'm afraid he's gone."

"No!" Emily drew in a hissing breath. "You're sure about that?"

Myrtle nodded. "Very sure. I'm so very sorry. What horrible news that must be for you."

Tears did indeed well in Emily's eyes. Myrtle realized she hadn't restocked her purse with tissue packets. Fortunately, Emily's complex coffee order arrived just at that moment, along with several napkins. Even more fortunately, Emily appeared to rally as her coffee was placed in front of her. She took a big sip and closed her eyes appreciatively.

"Well," she said, "Earl did have a good life. But I hate he died right when he was worried about getting landscaping work. His business really took a hit when Hortense fired him." She gave a short laugh. "Seems like everybody is getting fired these days." She looked at Myrtle. "Did he have a heart attack or something?"

"I'm afraid he was murdered. Taken before his time. It's a terrible thing."

Emily's eyes grew wide. Myrtle was relieved to see that there was no trace of tears in them this time, however. "What is going *on?*" asked Emily. "That's unbelievable. I mean, I could see somebody getting fed up with Hortense and killing her. But Earl? He was just this gruff but gentle guy. Loved being outside with plants. Who'd want to murder Earl?"

Myrtle said gently, "Apparently, the police aren't sure yet. Perhaps Earl knew something about Hortense's murder. Maybe the murderer felt they had to kill him in order to keep him from sharing what he knew."

Emily took a thoughtful sip of her coffee. "That makes at least a little sense. Somebody panicked and felt like they had to get rid of Earl. Still, that really shakes me up. When did this happen?"

"Yesterday morning. I'm surprised you didn't hear about it before now. You know how gossip spreads here in Bradley."

"Yes, I'm well-acquainted with that," said Emily dryly. "But no, I didn't hear about it. Yesterday morning, I'd just been fired by the diner. I showed up for work around nine because I'd overslept. They told me not to bother working my shift because they were letting me go. I left and went back home to touch up my resume. Then I went to the print shop to make copies of it."

Myrtle frowned. "You don't have a printer at home?"

Emily looked at Myrtle as if she were speaking a foreign language. "What? No, there's no room for a printer. And, really, I never need one, except for right now."

Myrtle nodded. It was a pity Emily didn't have an alibi for yesterday morning. Myrtle was rather fond of the hapless girl.

Emily rubbed her forehead. "I'm just having a tough time wrapping my head around the fact that Earl is gone. He was such a great guy to me."

"You said he was like a dad."

Emily grinned. "Yeah. Or maybe more of a granddad. I mean, he probably wasn't *old* enough to be my grandfather. But that's the kind of relationship that we had. He loved it when I came by his yard. He showed me all the different plants he had. It was like he was telling me a story of the plant's life. When I was over there, I felt like I was almost . . . home."

"That's wonderful. And great that Earl could open up his yard for you."

"He really did. Like I said, it felt like home. And Earl would never accuse me of trespassing like Hortense did." Her expression darkened, and she paused as she took another sip of her coffee. "My mother's garden was everything to me when I was a little girl. I remember long afternoons in the yard with her, pulling weeds and planting marigolds and other flowers."

Myrtle had a vague recollection of Emily's mother. "She was a single mom, wasn't she?"

Emily nodded. "Yes. She was all I had. Then she died of cancer when I was in middle school."

It was all coming back to Myrtle now. "I'm so sorry, my dear."

Emily sighed. "It was a long time ago. Anyway, I ended up with my aunt. I'm not saying I wasn't grateful to have a place to stay, but my aunt was totally disinterested in me. To be fair, she wasn't expecting to have a kid come stay with her. She took care of meals and a roof over my head, but she wasn't wanting to be a mom to me." She shrugged. "It's okay. I mean, it wasn't fun, but I made it through."

"Did your aunt have a yard at her house?" asked Myrtle.

Emily shook her head. "She rented her duplex. She didn't want me doing anything in the yard." She paused. "I really got into gardening again, though, when there was this free garden tour event."

"Oh, I remember that. A tour of yards. The garden club put that on months ago."

"Exactly," said Emily. "One house on the tour was Hortense's. She gave a talk and pointed out some things she was growing. I was so jealous. I wanted to head to the garden center and buy everything she told me about. But I knew I didn't have the money for it."

"Where are you living now?" asked Myrtle. "Not still with the evil aunt?" Myrtle didn't care for the sound of the aunt. It seemed she'd done the bare minimum to raise poor Emily.

"No, I'm renting my own place now. But the landlord is cool with my gardening. It's just that I can't afford to buy plants."

Myrtle considered this. "I'm not saying my yard is as remarkable as Hortense's. In fact, my prize rosebush has recently been decimated by a deer who wandered over from my neighbor's yard. But I have some heirloom plants. A lovely peony, some catmint, morning glories, and asters. You're more than welcome to come over at any time and divide them."

Emily gave her a delighted smile. "You mean it?"

"I certainly do. My yard is your yard. And I'm not like Hortense; I won't forget that I told you to come."

"Wow, that's awesome." Then, to Myrtle's horror, she broke down into those tears that she'd so far successfully avoided.

Myrtle stiffened. "There, there," she said, somewhat ineffectually. "You'll be all right, won't you?"

Emily used some of her napkins to dab at her face. "You're just so nice. Thanks, Miss Myrtle. And here I was thinking it was the worst day ever because of Earl dying." At the thought of Earl, Emily started boo-hooing once again.

"Maybe a restorative sip of your coffee, dear," suggested Myrtle in alarm.

Emily choked down her coffee in between sobs. Finally, settling down a bit, she said, "Hey, I just remembered—you work for the paper, don't you?"

"Does someone your age read the paper?"

Emily shook her head. "No, but I follow it on social media, so I get the headlines. I haven't been online today, but I saw your story on Hortense." She paused, dabbing at her face again. "You're being so nice to me that I'd like to tell you something in return."

Myrtle gave Emily an encouraging smile, since she seemed to have a hard time moving forward.

Emily took a deep breath. "Okay. I can do this." She looked around the coffeehouse to make sure no one was close enough to overhear her. "So, when Hortense lost it about me being in her yard, I got really worried. I knew she wasn't the kind of person to keep stuff to herself, and I figured there might be a lot of negative fallout if she started telling people I was stealing plants from her."

"And you *weren't* stealing plants."

"Exactly. Anyway, I did something I'm not proud of, Miss Myrtle. Hortense was working out in her yard, doing some weeding. I wasn't working that day. I decided to go inside Hortense's house, which was unlocked while she was outdoors."

Myrtle raised her eyebrows. "What were you hoping to find? Some dirt on Hortense?"

Emily looked relieved that Myrtle had put two and two together. "That's right. I wore latex gloves, just in case. I wasn't trying to rob her, you know. I just wanted to see if there was something there that I could hold against Hortense to make her stop talking about me. It's tough enough finding a job in this town without people calling you a thief. Anyway, while I was inside her house, I found her diary."

Now Myrtle's eyebrows were even higher. "Did you, now?"

Emily gave her a weak grin. "Yep."

"Remind me never to make an enemy of you, Emily," said Myrtle.

"Oh, no worries about that, Miss Myrtle. Anyway, I swiped the diary, thinking it might give me some info for blackmail."

Myrtle said, "You didn't think it might be a little late for that? Hortense had already started spreading the word about the incident, hadn't she?"

Emily shrugged. "Yeah. Even though she was trying really hard to destroy my reputation, I figured maybe Hortense could retract her allegation. Maybe she could show support of me somehow, and I could get my good reputation back."

Myrtle leaned over the table. "And what did you find in the diary?"

"Well, she was pretty mad at Harold. That's her ex-husband, you know. Hortense thought Harold was saying awful things about her. When they'd fight, he'd apparently throw out all these insults. She was furious with him over it. She divorced him right away."

Myrtle said, "But the divorce was a while back. Was there anything more recent in the diary?"

"She wrote in the diary every single day, even if it was just a couple of lines. Harold was *still* being ugly to her, just in the last couple of weeks. She said that his pride couldn't take it that Hortense had divorced him. Then she said something else." Emily paused. "She said she was going to make an appointment to change her will the very next week."

Myrtle and Emily sat still, staring at each other.

"Did it say anything about Hortense telling Harold that she was going to cut him out of her will?"

Emily nodded. "It sure did. She went right down to the hardware store during its busiest time and told Harold she was changing her will."

Myrtle said, "Well, that diary sounds like a keg of dynamite, Emily."

"Isn't it? I haven't known what to do. Before Hortense died, I thought of the diary as a tool to stop Hortense from talking. But now, I'm really worried about it. Here I am, trying to get a job." Emily gestured to the stack of resumes on the table. "And I've got a diary that I'm illegally in possession of. I've been making myself sick over it. If I give it to the cops, they're going to want to know how I got it. I could be arrested for trespassing and stealing and who knows what else."

Myrtle said, "Well, there's an easy solution to that. Give it to me and I'll plonk it down on Red's front porch in the middle of the night."

"That sounds like a lot of trouble for you, Miss Myrtle."

"Oh, no. I'm often up taking walks in the middle of the night. It's no trouble at all."

Emily said, "What if he catches you, though? He'll think *you* took the diary."

Myrtle waved her hand dismissively. "Don't worry about that, dear. Red sleeps like the dead. He won't catch me, I can promise you that."

Emily still looked worried. Myrtle said, "Even if he catches me, I'll just say I found the diary when I was visiting the public library. I opened it, realized it was Hortense's property, and left it on his doorstep. No problem."

Emily said slowly, "In that case, I'd really appreciate if you'd take it off my hands. Like I said, it's been worrying me day and night. I haven't been able to sleep with the diary in my house."

"Let's just set up a time for me to take it from you. I can get Miles to drive me if you don't live close."

Emily gave her a small smile. "No need to do that." She reached over and pulled a small red notebook from her purse. "Here's the diary."

Myrtle looked at it in surprise. "It's a lot slimmer than I thought it would be. In my head, I thought something that explosive should have a lock and key, at the very least."

Emily snorted. "I guess Hortense felt it was safe in her home."

"She certainly underestimated you," said Myrtle. She put the small notebook in her own purse and patted it. "It's safe and sound now."

Emily expelled a relieved sigh. "Thanks so much, Miss Myrtle. For the coffee, of course, and for taking that diary, too." She looked at her watch. "I'd better be going. I wanted to talk to the businesses before they got too busy."

"Good luck with your job search, dear."

After Emily walked out, Myrtle squinted at the check they'd been given for the coffees. Her eyes opened wide. She could have eaten an entire meal at the diner for what Emily's coffee cost. At least Emily had appeared to enjoy it.

Myrtle paid the formidable bill, relieved that she'd just been paid. She supposed she should run to the pharmacy while she was downtown, since she had a couple of things to pick up. She'd completely forgotten to get them in the rush to get poor Elaine's meds and Jack's lollipops. The pharmacy was also something of a hub for the town, at least for people of a certain age. As she recalled, they also stocked a bit of pet food on one aisle. Perhaps she could kill two birds with one stone.

When she walked into the drugstore, she immediately saw Martha Green speaking animatedly with Arthur Wilkins, the botanist. Arthur looked very much as if he wanted to be somewhere else entirely.

Myrtle was just thinking of ways she could interject herself in their conversation when Martha eagerly motioned her over.

"Help me persuade Arthur to be the head judge for the rescheduled show. He'll be perfect for it."

Arthur gave Myrtle a weary look. Then he said to Martha, "I'll think about it."

"Would you? Just call me anytime." She smiled at them both and then scampered off to the shampoo and conditioner aisle, not far away.

Myrtle sweetly said, "It's marvelous that I ran into you here. I've been thinking about you. You've been through such a stressful time, and now it appears you're going to be ensnared in the flower show."

Arthur gave her a grimacing smile. "Well, that's yet to be determined."

"I've been thinking about bringing by more food for you. Like I said, you've been through such a tough time."

Now Arthur looked alarmed. "That really won't be necessary. Aren't you very busy, anyway? I believe I've read some of your articles in the newspaper lately. They seemed very thorough."

"Aren't they?" asked Myrtle, beaming at him. "Of course, I'm always open to learning any new information about the cases. Consider me a hotline. I want to make sure I'm the one with the scoop. Do you have any tips for me?"

Arthur was looking longingly across the pharmacy, as if wishing he could teleport there. "No."

"Let me know if you hear anything. Even if it's just a human-interest angle for the stories I'll be writing. I could use more background on Earl for the profile piece I'll be doing. Since you're a botanist and Earl did landscaping work for you, do you know much about him?"

He gave her a tight smile. "I don't."

"Really? Not even about his plans to work for the botanical gardens near Charlotte? The Daniel Stowe gardens, aren't they?"

Arthur narrowed his eyes. "Earl didn't have the formal qualifications for that kind of work." He glanced nervously at Martha, still hovering nearby in the shampoo aisle, as if he thought she might start pressuring him to be a judge again.

"You might as well give in," said Myrtle.

Chapter Sixteen

Arthur looked startled. "Excuse me?"

"Give in to Martha. I know her—she won't give up. She's like a small terrier. She'll incessantly keep calling, emailing, and texting. Your life won't be your own anymore."

Arthur looked even grimmer. He appeared to be considering his options. "Okay, I'll do it," he grated. "Could you tell her? I don't want to get caught up in an interminable conversation with her again. I have things to pick up from the pharmacist." He hurried off to the back of the store toward the pharmacy counter.

Myrtle joined Martha in the shampoo aisle. "He'll do it," said Myrtle.

Martha gave a squeal. "You're a magician. I don't know how you did it."

"I don't know, either. He doesn't seem fond of flower shows. Judging one might prove rather excruciating."

Martha frowned. "Well, he was at the last one."

"He couldn't make it," said Myrtle. "He got caught up in re-search."

"No," insisted Martha. "He was there. I remember seeing him arrive and thinking that he looked defensive about being there. Like he wanted to avoid Hortense at all costs, since they'd just broken up. I thought it was quite brave that he'd shown up."

"That's very interesting," said Myrtle flatly.

Martha's mouth kept moving as she chatted more and more about the rescheduled flower show. Myrtle nodded from time to time, but her mind was on the suspects. Harold knew Hortense's will was going to be changed. Arthur was at the flower show. Emily had been sneaking around Hortense's house, so who knew what else she might be capable of? And Martha, who seemed so completely wrapped up in flower shows and creating horrible arrangements, appeared quite happy now that Hortense was gone for good.

When Martha finally paused to take a breath, Myrtle said, "I'm afraid I need to head back to my house after I pick up a couple of things here."

"Oh, I can drive you. You shouldn't have to walk home carrying a bag and your cane, too."

Myrtle paused. Did she really want to get in a car with Martha? She wasn't at all convinced that Martha wasn't a vicious murderer.

"No, dear, I think I'd rather stretch my legs a little. The bag won't be heavy at all. It was good talking to you, though," she fibbed as she walked farther into the store.

The sun shone brightly on her as she headed back home minutes later, purchases in hand. Myrtle absently wandered down the sidewalk, her thoughts a million miles away. She felt as if she needed to sit down in her living room and recalibrate everything she knew. Her head was fairly spinning with information.

Although she hadn't walked at a very fast pace, Myrtle was soon home. She sat down and took out a notebook. She wrote everyone's name in it, then stared at the names. There were actually a couple of excellent options for the role of murderer. Myrtle decided having a tomato sandwich might help her mental processes. But after eating one, she was still no closer to completely determining who the culprit might be. However, she had it narrowed down to two favorites—Harold and Arthur. Hortense's spurned loves.

Then she pulled out Hortense's diary, smiling to herself. It was nice to have such a thing. She could only imagine Hortense's face if she'd known Myrtle would end up reading her private thoughts.

Sadly, Hortense's diary appeared to be stultifyingly boring. It was often just lists of garden tasks. As Myrtle read further, she noted that Hortense could be quite a mean girl. She said disparaging things about Emily and how awful she was at waitressing. "Quite true," said Myrtle to herself. Still, the manner in which Hortense wrote about poor Emily was unnecessarily excoriating. What was worse was a passage in which Hortense wrote about the incident between Emily and herself in her yard.

Pretended to forget that I'd given permission for Emily to divide the Hostas and the giant fern. She looked so distressed and horrified when I came out and accused her of thievery. Perhaps I shouldn't have done it, but there's something about Emily that really bothers me. Maybe it's her talent and enthusiasm.

Myrtle made a face. At least Hortense was honest with herself. However, the person who was revealed was unbelievably obnoxious.

Myrtle continued scrolling through the little book, past tedious passages where Hortense duly recorded eating toast for breakfast, leftovers for supper, and recounted the weather for the day. Finally, she reached the part where Hortense talked about the auction Sloan had mentioned. Her account corroborated what Sloan had said.

Couldn't have been more delighted when I outbid Martha for that chef thing in LA. At first, I thought I'd just sell the package online since I don't give a whit about the chef, the food, or Los Angeles. Now, though, I've realized it'll be much better if I take the trip, photograph every second, and post it on my social media. Oh, getting it put in the newspaper will be perfect, too. Any opportunity to rub it in Martha's face. She's always so very annoying with her hideous flower arrangements.

Myrtle reflected Hortense was not the kindest of women. In fact, Myrtle could easily see how the world might be considered a brighter place without Hortense in it. However, this didn't mean that someone should kill with impunity. Whoever murdered Hortense and Earl needed to have their day in court.

Lastly, Myrtle found a recent entry in Hortense's diary, regarding the day she informed Harold she was writing him out of her will. And, presumably, dropping him as a beneficiary, since that appeared to be how Harold was going to be getting money in the near future.

Saw Harold in the street, sweeping outside the hardware store. I know I should have just passed by him without speaking, but something made me stop. Perhaps it was Harold's relaxed, jolly countenance. He never has to work at being happy, and that's very annoying. I told him I'd finally made an appointment with my attorney to change my will. It was nice to see the smile drop off his face. It wasn't because he was disappointed in not being a beneficiary—after all, he would have had no expectations of that following our divorce. I think what made him more unhappy was that my former landscaper, Earl, and my ex-beau, Arthur, overheard me. Harold does like to portray our divorce as amicable.

Myrtle concurred that Harold seemed to think a lot about how others viewed him. He certainly had plenty of motive. Perhaps he murdered Hortense not just to prevent her from changing her will and beneficiary designation, but because he was angry at the way she belittled him in front of others. It was all so very much to think about.

Her mind also drifted to poor Emily, and the girl's difficulty finding a job. Myrtle suddenly recalled that Tippy was extremely well-connected. Myrtle decided to call her again. "Tippy? It's Myrtle."

"Oh, Myrtle. Hi." She was quiet for a moment. "I'm afraid I really *don't* know anything else about memorial plans for Hortense."

"I'm actually calling on a different matter today, Tippy. Are you acquainted with Emily White?"

"The young woman who's so interested in horticulture. Yes, I do know her."

Myrtle reflected that it was fortunate that Tippy didn't seem to connect Emily with the diner. Perhaps she didn't know her disastrous employment history. "I know you're working on a scholarship for Wanda for garden club dues. Do you think the club could extend the same scholarship to Emily?"

Tippy paused. "I'd have to look at the books, but I don't see why not. Is Emily currently low on funds?"

"For any discretionary spending, yes. She just lost her job and seems to be having a difficult time finding another." Myrtle waited. If there was one thing Tippy couldn't resist, it was a problem to be fixed.

Sure enough, Tippy spoke right up. "Is she? I hate to hear that. She seems like such a promising young woman. I'm sure I could find her something."

"I don't suppose the garden center is hiring, is it?" asked Myrtle innocently. In the town of Bradley, nearly everyone was connected in a byzantine web of relations. She happened to know that one of Tippy's distant cousins owned the place.

"I haven't heard that they are, but I'm sure Penny could take Emily on. She's always complaining how overworked she is. Do you think it's the sort of job Emily would take to?"

Myrtle said, "Far better than an office job. In fact, I think Penny might have to push her out of the gate and lock it behind her just to make Emily go home at night."

Tippy laughed. "Got it. Well, consider it done. Penny owes me a few favors, and it sounds like a great time to call them in."

"Do you need Emily's contact information?" asked Myrtle. Not that she had it. But it seemed like the right thing to ask.

"No worries—I can find her online, I'm sure. I should run now. Bye, Myrtle."

Myrtle hung up, feeling pleased. It was nice to be doing something positive. She certainly hoped Emily didn't end up being the killer. Then her good deeds wouldn't seem quite so wonderful.

Myrtle reflected on her next move. She felt as if she needed to move around a little. Perhaps a bit of yardwork would help clear her head. It was a lovely day outside. But even better, Erma was off traveling. She could go outdoors, putter around, and contemplate murder. It seemed a very satisfactory plan.

After a moment of hesitation, she picked up the ergonomic yard tools she'd won at the flower show. Myrtle didn't *need* them, since she didn't have a single bit of arthritis. But she did so hate wasting perfectly good tools. They should at least get a little dirty. She made several trips from her outdoor shed to her yard, pulling out a gardening bench and a few other things. She might as well really get things done in the yard if she was going to be out there.

Minutes later, she was pruning her poor, deer-nibbled rosebush. "You'll get better, my dear," said Myrtle in a comforting manner.

After addressing the rosebush, she picked up her new ergonomic cultivator. There was a patch of chickweed that she wanted to attack. She was certain it had planted itself after being spawned in Erma's unkempt yard. All sorts of weeds found their origins there. She pushed the garden bench closer.

Which was when she heard a voice behind her.

Myrtle turned and glared coldly at Arthur Wilkins. "I don't recall inviting you in my backyard."

He gave her a wolfish smile. "I did knock at the front door, but you didn't hear me. I was concerned about you, so I walked around the back and check on you."

Myrtle raised her chin. "And as you can see, I'm hunky-do-ry."

"You don't seem thrilled to see me. Don't you like visitors?"

Myrtle said, "Perhaps I don't want a botanist wandering around my pitiful backyard. My roses have been decimated, and I'm trying to make everything tidier out here."

Arthur hesitated, seemingly uncertain about how to proceed.

"Did you want to ask me something?" asked Myrtle impatiently. Although ordinarily she would have appreciated the chance to speak with a suspect, his unexpected arrival in her backyard had unsettled her.

Arthur apparently figured out his path forward. "Yes. I suppose you were speaking with Martha Green about me after our conversation in the pharmacy."

"Oh, that. As you asked, I told Martha you agreed to be the grand judge for the flower show. We spoke of you, but only tangentially." Although she certainly hadn't picked up on Arthur being romantically interested in Martha, Myrtle wondered if they were about to have an extremely awkward moment where Arthur inquired whether Martha liked him. She had no desire to be in the middle of such a juvenile activity. However, that would be preferable to Arthur attempting to murder her in her own backyard. Which she increasingly feared might be the case.

"Martha said something about my being there, didn't she?" Arthur rattled off the words carelessly. Myrtle got the impression he was trying to see exactly what Myrtle knew, without revealing anything.

"Perhaps she did," said Myrtle with a shrug. "But perhaps not."

Arthur's lips curled. "I thought that might have been the case. I watched you coming out of the pharmacy, and I could tell you thought you knew something. You should know that Martha is very unreliable. Her head is in the clouds half the time. All she thinks about is those awful flower arrangements of hers."

Myrtle raised her eyebrows. "Point taken. Now, if you'd leave my yard. I have things to do."

Arthur's eyes narrowed. "You have quite a condemning expression on your face, Miss Myrtle."

"Don't feel flattered. I often wear a condemning expression. Perhaps I was thinking about Martha's flowers."

"I was curious what you knew about Earl's plans to leave Bradley," said Arthur. "As far as I was aware, he'd kept those plans to himself."

"Well, if *you* know about them," said Myrtle in an acerbic tone, "and if *I* know about them, that can't really be the case, can it?"

Arthur just waited for her to elaborate.

Myrtle huffed out an irritated sigh. "I had a conversation with Earl. He was interested in leaving Bradley, and why wouldn't he be? He'd lost customers lately, and Hortense was spreading all sorts of lies about him being incompetent. He clearly loved flowers. The botanical gardens sound like they would have been the perfect fit for him."

"Except that he was unqualified."

Myrtle frowned. "That's for the botanical gardens to decide, surely. Earl wasn't a naturalist or a horticulturist, but he would have made an excellent groundskeeper." After a moment or two, she said slowly, "You're likely connected with the gardens, aren't you? Considering you're a specialist. Have you done work there before?"

"I have," said Arthur stiffly. "Which is why I know Earl wouldn't have been qualified."

"Perhaps Earl needed a recommendation from you," continued Myrtle thoughtfully. "That would have really spoken well of him to the gardens. And perhaps you didn't want to give that recommendation. Just considering the way you're acting right now."

Arthur didn't answer.

Myrtle said slowly, "Perhaps Earl needed that recommendation so much that he blackmailed you to get it."

Myrtle knew for sure now. Arthur was there to silence her. Everything about his stance was threatening. And Myrtle shrilly yelled for help.

Arthur shrugged. "Knock yourself out. No one is around. There are no cars in any of the driveways. Go ahead and scream."

Chapter Seventeen

So Myrtle did. But she was perhaps louder than Arthur had anticipated. He snapped at her to shut her mouth and then lunged at her.

Unfortunately for Arthur, Myrtle still clutched her ergonomic garden fork. She stabbed him, without compunction, in his generous belly.

Arthur howled, then lunged again for her. But blinded by pain or rage, he seemed not to notice Myrtle's gardening bench. He tripped over it and went flying through the air. Myrtle ran as quickly as she could, clutching her cane, hurrying through the gate and into the front yard.

But Arthur was right. There were no cars to be seen. It was as if she and Arthur were the only people on the street. She recalled, belatedly, that Miles must be at chess club. Perhaps Elaine was fit enough to be running errands now that her neck had improved. And Erma, of course, was out of town. So Myrtle, who couldn't get into her locked front door, rounded the *other* side of the house and into her back door while Arthur was apparently chasing around to the front.

She bolted the back door behind her, panting. Myrtle could hear the door rattling at the front as Arthur tried to get in that way. He commenced a furious pounding on its frame.

There was a shout in the front; a man's voice, clipped and forceful. The pounding stopped.

"Mrs. Clover?" asked a familiar voice from the front porch. "Are you okay? Is this man bothering you?"

"Yes, he is!" A smile spread across Myrtle's features as she hurried to the front door. Lieutenant Perkins had perfect timing.

When she opened the door, Perkins had Arthur's hands behind him in handcuffs. Unlike Arthur and Myrtle, Perkins wasn't out of breath at all. But a broken lightbulb was scattered on her front walkway.

"My apologies for that," said Perkins smoothly, "I just came by to install a new lightbulb for you, since I noticed last night that it hadn't been changed out yet. And, while coming up your front walk, I couldn't help but notice this man trying to gain entry into your house. It appeared you didn't want him there."

"You are correct," said Myrtle. "Arthur Wilkins is the killer." She glared at Arthur, who scowled back.

Arthur said in an icy tone, "You should be arresting *her*. Have you even noticed my injury?"

Perkins said, "I've noticed blood coming out of the front of your shirt. Would it be all right, Mrs. Clover, if we went inside? I'll call an ambulance. I can promise you that you won't have any more trouble with this guy."

"Come on in. I may fix myself a wee glass of sherry."

Perkins said, "I'd do the same thing in your shoes."

Perkins pushed Arthur none too gently inside Myrtle's house and moved him to sit on her sofa. Then he made a few quick calls while Myrtle took out her diminutive crystal sherry glass and poured herself a small drink. Then she returned to the living room and sat herself in the armchair, sipping delicately.

Arthur was indeed bloody, although it didn't seem bad enough to do any serious damage—either to Arthur or to Myrtle's upholstery.

Perkins hung up his phone and informed Arthur of his rights. "Now, could I get an account of what happened?" He pushed a button on his cell phone that Myrtle assumed was a recorder.

Myrtle said primly, "I was gardening outside, minding my own business, when Arthur appeared. He lunged at me, and I stabbed him in the stomach with the ergonomic garden fork I won at the flower show."

Arthur snarled at her.

Myrtle ignored him, as did Perkins. Perkins asked, "Why did Arthur lunge at you?"

Arthur interrupted, "Because she was getting involved in other people's business."

Myrtle raised an eyebrow at him. "Temper, temper." She turned to Perkins. "The problem is that Arthur quickly has the ability to see red. That's what I believe happened when Hortense broke up with him. It made him seethe. Regardless of what he's told you, Arthur was at the flower show the morning Hortense died. Martha Green will tell you she saw him there."

Perkins said to Arthur, "Did you attend the flower show with the express purpose of killing Hortense?"

"I didn't," growled Arthur.

Myrtle considered the man thoughtfully. "As a matter of fact, I don't believe Arthur *did* plan on killing Hortense. He'd have arrived at the venue far better prepared than he was. Hortense wouldn't have been murdered by a flowerpot; she'd have been killed with an actual weapon, instead. I think he simply wanted to be there to tell her off. Perhaps he wanted to interrupt her in the middle of her judging duties and distract her from her task. But something went haywire. Most likely Hortense, an acerbic woman at the best of times, gave him a piece of her mind. Or belittled him. I don't believe Arthur would take kindly to being belittled. He's awfully fond of his role as expert."

There was a distant wail of a siren. Then another.

Perkins leaned forward. "And Earl Jenkins?"

"Poor Earl had a gift for being in the wrong place at the wrong time. Hortense and her ex-husband, Harold, were having an argument in the middle of downtown just recently. Hortense was fed-up with Harold and told him she was planning on changing her will." Myrtle carefully didn't mention that the information had come from the diary Emily stole. She looked over at Arthur. "Arthur overheard Hortense's threat. Of course, Arthur wasn't planning on *murdering* Hortense. Like we said, the murder was more of a result of Arthur not having full control of his temper."

The sirens came closer. Perkins said, "But it seemed an excellent red herring to make the police think Harold was responsible. He certainly had an excellent motive."

"Yes. The problem was, however, that Harold claimed he did not know that Hortense was planning on changing her will.

He'd thought she'd changed it directly after their divorce, which would have made the most sense. But Hortense apparently had a habit of procrastinating administrative tasks," said Myrtle.

Perkins said thoughtfully, "As a matter of fact, we received an anonymous email from someone following Hortense's death, saying they'd overheard Hortense's threat. It stated that Harold was aware that Hortense was planning on changing the will. The email address was clearly an alias. I very much wonder if we'll find that account on your device, Mr. Wilkins."

Arthur seemed even angrier than he was before. Myrtle fully expected to see steam coming out of his ears soon.

Perkins continued, "If we could go back to Earl Jenkins, now."

"Oh, that's right. That was your original question. From the information I received, Hortense and Harold didn't have a private conversation about the will. Instead, it was done in a public place with a couple of people listening in. I'm sure they were listening quite avidly, considering the topic. One of them was Arthur, who later used the information to send you on the red herring regarding Harold's motive. The other was poor Earl. Arthur remembered Earl taking note of the argument. Earl must have also registered that Arthur was there, overhearing it all."

Arthur's gaze was icy as Myrtle turned toward him. "Arthur, I'm assuming you went over to Earl's house for a friendly visit. You knew Earl wasn't fond of speaking on phones."

"A ridiculous thing for someone running his own business," muttered Arthur.

Myrtle said, "You weren't originally planning on sending an anonymous email to the police, were you? I bet you were at

Earl's house trying to persuade him to tell the police what he'd overheard. You must have reminded him he was a witness to Hortense's threats against Harold. I'm guessing Earl probably told you that you should simply tell the police yourself. You'd been there, too."

Myrtle stared at Arthur until he shrugged. "I told Earl I was too close to Hortense for the police to believe me. It would look as if I was shifting blame to Harold. It seemed to me that it would be more believable coming from somebody like Earl."

Perkins said, "But Earl had his own reasons for wanting Hortense gone. Did you push Earl to report what he'd heard? Did Earl become suspicious of your real reasons for wanting him to come forward?"

Arthur looked sullenly at him.

Myrtle said, "Arthur decided it made sense to kill Earl just to make sure he didn't cause any trouble. The last thing Arthur wanted was for Earl to report *him* to the police instead of Hortense's threats against Harold." She raised her eyebrows at Arthur. "When I came across Arthur earlier today, I told Arthur he'd been spotted at the flower show, even though he'd denied being there. I also dropped in conversation that I knew Earl wanted to work at the botanical gardens near Charlotte."

"Earl was planning on leaving town?" asked Perkins.

"That's right. Hortense's gossip had made his landscaping business take a hit. Being investigated as a suspect in her murder likely didn't help, either. Arthur became suspicious when I asked him if Earl had spoken with Arthur about the botanical gardens. I only asked because I knew Arthur probably had connections there. But judging from Arthur's reaction, I'm guessing that Earl was trying to blackmail Arthur into getting him a job at the gardens. Earl must have told Arthur that he'd tell the police about Arthur's erratic behavior. That meant Earl had to die, and I suppose that's why Arthur came for me this afternoon, too. Apparently, Arthur's ultimately ineffective strategy was to kill everyone who might be suspicious of his involvement."

The paramedics came rushing in. Arthur looked at them with relief. But the paramedics were quickly followed by Red and members of the state police.

The paramedics examined Arthur's stab wounds, which appeared to have bled a bit, but weren't serious.

"Self-defense," said Myrtle curtly as Red shot her a questioning look.

Red dropped next to Perkins on the sofa. "You're alright?" he asked his mother.

"Never better," said Myrtle firmly. "It's always glorious to be alive when one escapes with one's life."

"Of course, one shouldn't be in that predicament to begin with." Red rubbed his face with both hands, gazing at his mother with tired eyes.

"Oh, before I forget, I should give you this." Myrtle reached into a drawer and tossed Hortense's small diary to Red.

Red frowned at the book. "What's this?"

"You'll find it's Hortense Winston's diary. It's quite illuminating in spots. In other spots, it's dreadfully dull."

Red and Perkins looked at each other. Red said, "Mama, how did this come to be in your possession?"

"Quite by chance. I'm not at liberty to go into details. Suffice it to say that I acquired it. And now I'm relinquishing it."

Red rubbed his temples. "Okay. And how did Arthur Wilkins end up trying to murder you in your backyard?"

Myrtle took a sip of her sherry. "I just filled in Perkins completely. I'm positive he'll do a wonderful job recounting everything."

"You don't have the time to repeat it?" asked Red in a doubtful tone.

"I don't. I'm planning on enjoying myself today by having Miles take me up to see Wanda. He should be home from his chess club soon. Wanda's been working hard in her garden, and I'd like to see it."

Perkins said, "That sounds like an excellent way to spend the day, Mrs. Clover."

"It does, doesn't it? Thanks again for rescuing me, Lieutenant."

Perkins shook his head. "You did a fine job of rescuing yourself."

"And Arthur has the stab wounds to prove it," said Red with a snort.

Soon, everyone cleared out of Myrtle's small house. She finished her sherry while typing up an exclusive article for Sloan.

She'd just emailed the story to Sloan when there was a knock at her door. When she opened it, Miles stood there, frowning. "I heard what happened while I was at chess club."

"How on earth did the news reach the inner sanctums of your chess club that quickly? Never mind, I know Bradley's gossip works in mysterious ways."

Miles studied his friend, his expression concerned. "Well, you certainly look like you got out unscathed."

"Completely. It was a bit traumatic while it was happening, but all's well that ends well. Arthur was arrested. I'm sure he'll spend quite a long time behind bars for two homicides and plans for a third. Good riddance." Myrtle paused. "Now to more exciting things."

"More exciting than eluding murderers?"

"Maybe *exciting* isn't the right word. Now to more *pleasant* things. That works better," said Myrtle.

"Such as?"

"Let's visit Wanda. There's something calming about being at Wanda's hubcap-covered shack, isn't there?"

Miles appeared to disagree. He patted the pocket of his khaki pants to ensure his bottle of hand-sanitizer was there.

"I'll give her a quick call to make sure she's there," said Myrtle. "Now that she has her new phone, courtesy of her wildly wealthy client, communication is certain to be easier."

Miles was still stuck on the fact that Myrtle wanted to call ahead. "Where else *would* Wanda be? If she's not there, she's here."

Myrtle ignored him and proceeded to make the phone call, putting it on speaker.

Wanda picked right up. "Wanna come visit?"

"I certainly do. Are you going to be around?"

"Sure will." Wanda paused. "Took care of the bad guys agin, didn't you?"

"I did," said Myrtle in a satisfied voice.

"Got some news for you."

Myrtle said, "I certainly hope it's good news. Today is a day for good news."

Myrtle could hear Wanda's grin when she spoke. "Dan is movin' out."

Miles gave an immediate, delighted thumbs-up.

"Moving *out*?" said Myrtle. "But that's wonderful! You'll have the whole place to yourself. How did this miraculous news come about?"

Wanda said, "He's gettin' hitched."

"*Married*? Crazy Dan?" This boggled Myrtle's mind. How did Dan even meet someone? Why would anyone *want* to marry him? Miles looked equally stumped.

"Yep. I wuz surprised, too." Wanda paused. "Mebbe that's what them visions was tellin' me. That Dan is gonna have a new beginnin'."

"It certainly sounds that way. Drinking coffee in a new kitchen, I believe you said?"

Wanda said, "That's right. Mebbe he'll like coffee now, jest because she does."

"Well, we now have all sorts of things to celebrate! Miles and I will be there with bells on." Myrtle hung up. "Can you imagine it?"

"I sure can't. But it's great news for Wanda. No more of Dan's hoarding. No more getting her bank account drained by Dan's constant online purchasing." A smile spread across Miles's features. The part about Wanda's healthier bank account seemed to make him especially pleased.

Thirty minutes later, they were at Wanda's house. Myrtle had wanted to concoct a dessert to bring to Wanda, but Miles, cognizant of the recent lemon souffle disaster, persuaded her to pick up fudge from the grocery store. Wanda appeared to be delighted by it.

Wanda ushered them into the shack, which had already undergone a dramatic change. Myrtle and Miles looked around in amazement. They could see all the various surfaces in the house, including the floor. Everything was neat and tidy and recently scrubbed clean. Wanda had removed the dark curtains at the windows and sunlight streamed in. She had various ivies, pothos, violets, and succulents sitting on the windowsills.

"It looks wonderful in here," breathed Myrtle.

Even Miles didn't make his customary grab for his hand sanitizer.

Wanda beamed happily at them. "It feels so much bigger."

Miles asked, "What are you going to do with the extra space?"

Wanda said shyly, "Might make an office outta Dan's room. My customer gave me lotsa stuff." She walked them into a back room where there was a fancy desktop computer, two monitors, an external microphone, and a webcam.

Miles gave a low whistle.

"And the internet?" asked Myrtle. "Did your client set you up with a better connection?"

Wanda nodded, giving them her gap-toothed grin. "Wanted to pay fer everything."

"Well, that's what happens when you provide a valuable service for someone." Myrtle looked around her with satisfaction. "This all makes me very happy, Wanda."

"Me, too. Lemme show you outside. Wanna give you two somethin.'"

Wanda led them into the backyard. She had a small, but flourishing garden, despite the unforgiving red clay soil and relentless sun. It mostly comprised of vegetables, but there also some pretty daylilies and knockout roses.

Wanda stooped to pick up two paper bags. She handed one to Myrtle and one to Miles. She cleared her throat. "Them are daylilies that I divided up. They was my mama's." She cleared her throat again. "They make me smile when I'm out here. Wanted to make y'all smile, too."

Myrtle found herself tearing up, which in Myrtle's eyes was unforgiveable. Even Miles gave a small sniff.

Before they all dissolved into tears, Myrtle said briskly, "Thank you, Wanda. This means so much to Miles and me. We know the high regard you hold your mama in." She took a steadying breath. "And now, I think it's time for fudge."

And so the three friends sat at a small table in Wanda's living room, happily eating fudge and talking about flowers and murder.

About the Author

Elizabeth writes the Southern Quilting mysteries and Memphis Barbeque mysteries for Penguin Random House and the Myrtle Clover series for Midnight Ink and independently. She blogs at ElizabethSpannCraig.com/blog, named by Writer's Digest as one of the 101 Best Websites for Writers. Elizabeth makes her home in Matthews, North Carolina, with her husband. She's the mother of two.

Sign up for Elizabeth's free newsletter to stay updated on releases:

https://bit.ly/2xZUXqO

This and That

I love hearing from my readers. You can find me on Facebook as Elizabeth Spann Craig Author, on Twitter as elizabethscraig, on my website at elizabethspanncraig.com, and by email at elizabethspanncraig@gmail.com.

Thanks so much for reading my book...I appreciate it. If you enjoyed the story, would you please leave a short review on the site where you purchased it? Just a few words would be great. Not only do I feel encouraged reading them, but they also help other readers discover my books. Thank you!

Did you know my books are available in print and ebook formats? Most of the Myrtle Clover series is available in audio and some of the Southern Quilting mysteries are. Find the audiobooks here: https://elizabethspanncraig.com/audio/

Please follow me on BookBub for my reading recommendations and release notifications.

I'd also like to thank some folks who helped me put this book together. Thanks to my cover designer, Karri Klawiter, for her awesome covers. Thanks to my editor, Judy Beatty for her help. Thanks to beta readers Amanda Arrieta, Rebecca Wahr, Cassie Kelley, and Dan Harris for all of their helpful suggestions and careful reading. Thanks to my ARC readers for helping to spread the word. Thanks, as always, to my family and readers.

Other Works by Elizabeth

Myrtle Clover Series in Order (be sure to look for the Myrtle series in audio, ebook, and print):

Pretty is as Pretty Dies

Progressive Dinner Deadly

A Dyeing Shame

A Body in the Backyard

Death at a Drop-In

A Body at Book Club

Death Pays a Visit

A Body at Bunco

Murder on Opening Night

Cruising for Murder

Cooking is Murder

A Body in the Trunk

Cleaning is Murder

Edit to Death

Hushed Up

A Body in the Attic

Murder on the Ballot

Death of a Suitor

A Dash of Murder
Death at a Diner
A Myrtle Clover Christmas
Murder at a Yard Sale
Doom and Bloom
A Toast to Murder (2024)
Southern Quilting Mysteries in Order:
Quilt or Innocence
Knot What it Seams
Quilt Trip
Shear Trouble
Tying the Knot
Patch of Trouble
Fall to Pieces
Rest in Pieces
On Pins and Needles
Fit to be Tied
Embroidering the Truth
Knot a Clue
Quilt-Ridden
Needled to Death
A Notion to Murder
Crosspatch
Behind the Seams
Quilt Complex
The Village Library Mysteries in Order:
Checked Out
Overdue
Borrowed Time

Hush-Hush
Where There's a Will
Frictional Characters
Spine Tingling
A Novel Idea
End of Story
Booked Up (2024)
Memphis Barbeque Mysteries in Order (Written as Riley Adams):
Delicious and Suspicious
Finger Lickin' Dead
Hickory Smoked Homicide
Rubbed Out
And a standalone "cozy zombie" novel: Race to Refuge, written as Liz Craig

Printed in Great Britain
by Amazon

33881837R00126